THE HANDS OF ONAN

Chris DiLeo

Also by Chris DiLeo

Onan's brother died and, as the ancient custom prescribed, Onan married his brother's wife but when he went in unto her, he removed himself and spilled his semen on the ground. This so angered the Lord he slew Onan.

—The Book of Genesis (paraphrased)

And when Onan was dead and cast into Hell, the Devil rose him up once more to be a god for all men who take their manhood in hand and worship their own pleasure.

—The Book of Onan (paraphrased)

This one is for you, brave reader. Thank you and enjoy!

ONE

I'VE ALWAYS BEEN A MASTURBATOR.

What guy isn't? Even those religious types in short sleeve white dress shirts take one hand off the Bible to give their meat a tug. Hell, maybe they do it *when* reading the Bible. *If thou be man, worship thyself with lube and palm.* That's the Gospel According to JackOff.

From the first time we discover how good it feels to stroke the salami, we're always thinking about doing it. This never goes away.

To cope with their stress, the brokers on Wall Street might escape to the bathroom stall several times a day to jerk it, and I bet E.R. doctors do the same thing, along with anyone else in a high-stress career.

The worst offenders, however, are creative types. Actors. Painters. And writers. Writers being the most habitual masturbators. I should know. I'm a writer. You don't know me or probably any of my work, but *Publisher's Weekly* once wrote of my novel that "Michael Stiffe aspires toward the literary perversions of a Roth or an Updike or even an Irving, yet resigns himself comfortably to being merely perverted."

That's framed on my office wall.

Like a narcissist jerking it to his own picture, I've masturbated in front of that quote many, many times.

That's odd, I know, and feel free to judge all you want, but it's like porn tailor-made for me and it gives me a strange sort of power.

At least that's what I tell myself.

I was once invited to write an essay on any aspect of writing I wanted for a collection of such essays, and I wrote about masturbating. "Taking Your Writing in Hand," I titled it.

My bio for the article read, "Michael Stiffe is a critically acclaimed literary writer who makes masturbation part of his daily writing process."

The article was not accepted for publication.

What can I say? As with any writing advice, there's always the caveat "Use what works for you."

If I'm going to be completely honest, besides the obvious that masturbation feels good—it's about boredom and frustration. The agony of creation. Say a story I'm writing isn't going well, so I pull out my dick and try to rediscover some enthusiasm. Or at least a momentary distraction.

Does a female writer dive a hand into her crotch when suffering the tedium of flaccid imagination? I don't know and it doesn't matter.

Not for this story, anyway.

What matters is simply this: I'm a masturbator, and it almost killed me.

When thou take thyself in hand, be thou dutiful yet aware for danger lurks everywhere.

So reads The First Letter of Mike to the Masturbators.

TWO

I WAS SUFFERING WRITER'S BLOCK, and instead of dwelling on the work joining all the other unfinished stories and novels I'd failed to complete, I decided to masturbate. I was getting ready when the doorbell rang.

It wasn't yet eight in the morning, I wasn't expecting any visitors, and I was standing in my office with my pants and boxers at my ankles, assorted adult pictures on my computer screen, and a glob of pine-scented moisturizer in my hand.

Maybe whoever it was would simply go away. Could be a religious guy. They could proselytize about the sin of self-pleasure. Or it could be a community member gathering signatures on a petition to ban whatever liberal ethos-indoctrinating book was now being taught at the high school. Maybe a book about self-pleasure. They'd leave a *Watchtower* or a flyer and be on their way.

The doorbell ding-donged again.

Even so, I almost jerked off anyway. I could be done in thirty seconds, if I wanted.

Hold your applause.

I wiped the moisturizer-gunk off my hand with the tissues I had

3

at the ready for my home-brewed gunk, pulled my pants up, and answered the door.

It was Elizabeth Delrose, my friend's wife.

For a three-second beat, she eyed me with knowing suspicion and I tucked my hands into my pockets as if their existence was proof of what I'd been about to do. We men may masturbate all the time, it's an understood non-secret and one we joke about frequently, but we still suffer shame when caught.

"Michael," she said, "I need your help."

"Sure," I said. "Is Drew okay?"

She stood almost perfectly still but I felt her jittery panic. It emanated off her like static electricity, threatening to zap me. She started to speak and a souped-up, piss-yellow hatchback sped past, its sport muffler screaming. Teenager, most likely. They were always speeding down my road and making sure everyone knew it.

"Can I come in?"

I stepped back and she entered. I shut the door against the spring morning, rain clouds beginning to clot the sky over the suburban New York neighborhood.

She went directly into the kitchen, I followed, and she spun around so suddenly I almost bumped into her.

"When was the last time you spoke to Drew?"

"Uh—a few days ago, I think."

"You actually spoke?"

She didn't let me answer.

"What was it?"

"What was—"

"*Tell me.*"

"It was nothing. I don't know what you think he—"

"There's no point lying to me," she said. "Don't try to protect him, 'bro code,' or some stupid nonsense. I *know* what he's doing."

That buzzing static electricity energy I sensed was not panic but anger.

"Wait, wait," I said, my hands out of my pockets and held up as if in surrender. She looked at my palms and scowled. Could she smell the moisturizer? "What exactly is going on?"

She huffed like a bull and tugged up the sleeves of her baggy GAP sweatshirt. "He joined a masturbation cult."

That should've been the punchline but there wasn't any joke.

"What?" I asked.

Elizabeth turned, paced a few steps, and turned back. Her short black hair whipped across her face. She was a beautiful woman and her anger magnified that beauty, smoothing her face into shiny rock. "This is all your fault," she said. "And *that's* why you're going to help me."

"My fault? Wait—masturbation cult?"

"Remember that sex book he was writing? He came to you because you're the literary pervert or whatever you call yourself. You gave him somebody's name for 'research.' That led to this. It's *your* fault."

"That was a while ago," I said.

Drew and I had been well into a session of scotch and beer—a thing we did every couple of months and after which my head would always throb for days and my gut would perpetually burp out sour belches—and it was getting late when he said he wanted to write THE sex book. It'd be a unique blend of fiction and nonfiction, sex advice but also stories to get you in the mood. And he wanted it to be a *respected* thing, the *ultimate guide*, so he was asking me for experts he could consult to give the work credibility.

"I gave him the name of a sex therapist."

"I almost called Catherine," she said. "But the last thing she'd want is to talk about you and sex."

"You're probably right."

Elizabeth stared at me, unblinking. My gut felt hollow, the way it did after those scotch sessions. My hands found their way back into my pockets.

"She said you wouldn't fuck her anymore."

"That's not . . ." *True*, is what I was about to say but thankfully stopped myself.

"All you did was *masturbate*," Elizabeth said.

That word an accusation. A conviction.

"It's not a . . ."—*addiction*, I thought—"it's a . . ."

"A what? A part of your writing process? Have you even finished a second book, yet?"

The comment stung because she was right—not only hadn't I successfully finished a follow-up to my only novel, I no longer had a publisher or an agent.

"At least Catherine never had a kid with you."

I might wonder what I'd done to deserve such abuse, but she was being completely upfront about it. Challenging me to defend myself because she knew I couldn't.

"Hold on," I said. "Where's Drew? What's going on?"

"I told you. He's joined some jerk-off cult or something."

"You're saying . . . ?"

"Yes. An actual cult where a bunch of men touch themselves."

I tried to find words or force a laugh but I couldn't do either.

"He's been gone three days," she said.

"Missing?"

"Are you listening to me?"

"I'm trying to make sense of this."

"You gave him the name of some sex therapist and now he's left me to join a masturbation cult. Clear enough for you?"

"You think he's left you?"

"I know he has."

"He told you?"

Another bull-like huff and she yanked her phone from the back pocket of her jeans. She tapped it several times and turned it to face me.

A video was playing.

It was dark and shaky, the sounds of people in the background, talking, moving around, and then Drew's face filled the screen. He was holding the phone slightly below his chin, making his balding head bulbous and alien.

Out of the din around him came a rising hum, like a chorus warming up.

"I'm sorry," he said. "I know you think this is crazy, or I'm crazy, or both, but it's not. It's *not*. I have to do this. There's magic here."

He was calm yet wired, more focused than usual, actually. For a guy who was always interrupting himself mid-sentence to interject whatever spontaneous thought, related or not, that had announced itself in his mind, a nervous-tic sort of thing, here he was composed, focused, sharp.

He's on drugs, I thought. *Adderall maybe.*

I'm onto something, he'd said to me.

Yeah, drugs.

Someone in that room moaned. Orgasmic?

"There's something real here," Drew said. "*Alive.*"

A man passed behind him, moving mechanically, robot-like.

He was naked and visibly aroused.

That strange humming sound got louder and louder. Drew turned his head toward the sound the way a dog does.

"Gotta go."

The image tilted down fast and Drew's erection was the only thing on the screen. He was stroking himself slowly. He'd been doing it this whole time. He was wearing some sort of full-body black cloak and it was bunched around his privates. His bare legs were startlingly white and hairless. A sourness hollowed my stomach. The image swooped back up to his face before I even had a chance to look away.

"This *isn't* a sex thing," he said, breathing faster, making static on the recording. He brought the camera toward his face. "There is no sex. Masturbation is not sex. This is so much more powerful."

The phone was so close to his face now he was a nose and a single eye.

"I'm not coming back." He swallowed as if about to cry. "I really did love you and Wes."

His pupil was so large it eclipsed his blue iris.

Not Adderall—cocaine. Or something stronger.

The video ended there, frozen on his black eye.

Elizabeth looked as if she might throw the phone.

"What about the police?" I asked.

It was all I could say. I mean, what the fuck, right? A masturbation cult? Yet it wasn't about sex? Then what was it about? What was the "so much more powerful" thing?

"Screw the police," she said. "I already went to them. Showed them this video. You know what they said? He's not in danger. Not being held against his will. They were trying not to laugh. You know what else they told me? 'Maybe he's turned gay.' 'Turned gay,' that's what they said."

"They said that?"

She was shaking her head.

"Maybe he's on drugs," I said. "Cocaine? Hallucinogenics?"

"No."

"It's got to be something," I said. "Has he been acting weird lately?"

"No."

"More distant than he usually is?"

"What'd he say to you?"

"Nothing."

I'm onto something. It's big, big.

"He hasn't been depressed or anything? I know he gets moody."

"Shut up," she said.

"What?"

"You don't get to question me. Did I turn my husband gay? Was he using drugs without me realizing? Was he depressed? Bullshit questions. That isn't what this is about."

"What is it about?"

"He doesn't get to run off," she said, voice rising. "I don't care if he's stressed or having a mental breakdown or exploring his sexuality. He doesn't have the right to do whatever *he* wants. Whatever *this* is." She shook the phone and stomped one foot. "*We have a child!*"

That child was Wes, an eight-year-old who liked baseball and video games. Drew loved his son but he never talked about him much one way or the other.

I really did love you and Wes.

"Men in their forties," she said, shaking her head, sounding almost completely calm. "Midlife crisis. Get a sports car. Have an affair. Lose all your savings on one spin of the roulette wheel in Vegas. No, my husband does *this*."

"A mental collapse," I said. "Sudden onset. I'm sure it happens."

"Oh, are you *sure* it happens?"

"Sorry, I'm as confused as you are."

"*Christ!*" This time she made as if to really hurl the phone onto the floor but released a scream instead. It was brief, a second or two, but loud enough to hurt my ears and keep reverberating around the kitchen for a few more seconds.

I took several steps back.

"Why can't he just fuck some twenty-something?" she said. "I could accept that. But this? It isn't even *Eyes Wide Shut* shit. Rich guys in masquerade costumes fucking gorgeous women. That makes sense. This? *No.* This is sad-sack losers stroking themselves like it's some stupid fraternity pledge challenge. And no, he hasn't lost his mind. He's just being a fucking idiot."

I was scared she might attack me. Genuinely. The anger might have momentarily enhanced her beauty, but now her right eye was bloodshot, blue veins flexed up her forehead, and her lips were stretched back so thin they were rubber bands about to snap.

"Look," I said, "let's take a breath and—"

She stomped toward me, shoved a finger at my face.

"Why don't you try giving a shit about someone else for once instead of only caring about your writing—or your dick." Pinkish drool

8

slipped onto her chin. She'd bitten the inside of her cheek or her tongue. "You're going to find him," she said. "Find him and bring him back."

slipped part her ahe? She'd clench the fistful, her cruel, or her command "you're going to fuck him," he said, "and him and him."
fumbled.

THREE

THERE WOULDN'T HAVE BEEN ANY point in protesting or challenging or negotiating with Elizabeth. I had given the name of a sex therapist to Drew and now he had joined some masturbation cult. The least I could do was question the therapist. My friendship and my responsibility compelled me to do that much.

With a little ironic luck, maybe it would be a dead end and I would be off the hook.

Is that shameful? Sure, but all I can do is shrug.

The sex therapist was located in what resembled a housing development or maybe a shopping center where all the buildings were identical and only the unique signage above the entrances distinguished one place from another.

I'd called ahead to make an appointment and spoken to Tina, the receptionist.

"Oh, Mr. Stiffe," she said, pronouncing it *stiffy* instead of the correct *Sty-fee*. "Long time."

"Yeah, well, I'd like to come in."

I heard her mouse-clicking. "It's been over a year."

"Yes," I said.

"Marcia has openings next Wednesday and Friday—"

"I need sooner. I need today, actually."

"Is this an emergency?" She said it in an almost flirtatious way that struck me as incredibly inappropriate. No one was calling a sex therapist in an emergency, and yet when it comes to sex it all sort of feels like an emergency, if that makes sense.

Or maybe she was just flirting with me.

"Can she see me?" I asked.

"She has no appointments today. Sorry, Mike."

"I don't need an appointment."

"Oh?"

"Just a few minutes to talk."

"Which is an appointment."

"It's not about me. It's about someone else."

"Girlfriend?"

Christ, she *was* flirting.

"No, this is about a friend. He's missing and I think Marcia spoke with him."

"Missing? Are you working for the police?"

"Look, I'm coming in. Just tell her. I need five minutes."

There was a lengthy pause and the sounds of more mouse-clicking. "Eleven-thirty," she said. "Catch her just before lunch."

I parked and got out of my car. My timing was so lucky, for me anyway. I spotted Dr. Marcia Howler heading to her own car for lunch and hurried after her.

The day was cool and getting cooler, rain clouds congregating like military forces readying to attack.

"Marcia!" I called.

She looked at me and glanced away, and I had a distinct feeling she was going to make a dash for her car. She'd lock herself inside it and I'd be knocking on the glass and trying to stay calm as I begged her for just a few minutes of her time and then she'd start the car and back out so fast she'd almost run over my foot.

That's a writer's imagination for you. At least it didn't involve masturbation.

"Michael," she said and sighed. "How are you?"

"Good, good, good," I said in one breath. "Tina tell you I called?"

"She did, yes." Dr. Howler was short and slender, always in a black or brown business suit tailored to her frame, and matching flats. No high heels or skirts for her, but it didn't matter—I'd developed all

11

sorts of imaginative scenarios about her body. Call me perverted (*Publisher's Weekly* did!), but most men acquire mental images of every woman they meet, storing up a trove of curves and skin to be recalled during onanistic throes.

"Can we talk? Only take a minute."

"I'm surprised," she said. "What was it you said at our last session, our *final* session? Oh, yes, you called me a 'self-righteous cun—'"

"I'm sorry," I blurted. I was, too. "I know what I said, but that was because of Catherine, not you."

"It was because of your unresolved issues," she said.

"Yes, fine, yes. I agree. I just need to ask you a quick—"

"If you want an appointment, maybe I can fit—"

"No, no, no, this isn't about me." I sounded a bit frantic. Elizabeth's bloodshot eye and pulsing forehead veins loomed over me as their own sort of threatening clouds. I needed to get some answers, a lead at least to get Elizabeth off my case.

Wow, a voice I thought of as Sarcastic Sam said in my mind. *You're such a great friend.*

Dr. Howler crossed and then uncrossed her arms. "Okay, Michael, what is it?"

"A friend of mine was writing a book about sex and I gave him your name. His name is Drew Delrose. Tall guy, skinny, bald, bit depressive. Did he come see you?"

"You know I can't talk about patients. You know that *distinctly*."

There was judgment in that word but I was guilty. I'd tried several times to get her to tell me what Catherine had said about me—*She call me a weirdo or something? Why, Dr. Howler said, do you think you're a weirdo?*

"He wasn't a patient, at least I don't think so. He was doing research."

"I don't remember," she said.

"Would've been sometime in the past several months. You have a good memory."

Her expression said she found that condescending. Perhaps it was.

"How's the masturbation addiction?" she asked.

"Under control, thanks," I said, thinking, *Most days I only do it three times, but some writing sessions demand a few extra wanks—four, five, even six times.*

"I'm on lunch, Mike."

"He definitely came here," I said. "Right? Tell me that. Please."

Her hesitation confirmed my hope.

"Yes," she said. Her shoulders dropped and she seemed to deflate an inch or two. "He came here, we spoke briefly, and he left."

"What'd he ask you?"

She was thinking.

"Any weird questions?"

"What happened?" she asked. "You wouldn't be asking me unless something happened."

His pupils enlarging to block out the blue of his eyes just as the clouds above obscured the sun.

"He's joined a cult. A masturbation cult."

She did not, of course, laugh (in her line of work, she'd heard plenty of far crazier sex tales), but something registered in her expression. *Recognition,* I thought.

"You know something," I said. "Tell me."

She started speaking and stopped herself, considering.

A breeze pushed over us. The back of my neck prickled.

"Either you tell me or his wife is going to come here and she *will* get answers. One way or another."

Playing the tough guy was never my strong suit, but I thought I did it well.

"Threatening me is maybe not the best way to proceed, Michael."

She regained those deflated inches.

So much for being a tough guy.

"I'm trying to help my friend."

"Sounds like it's his wife you're helping."

Was that an intimation? Was she implying something?

"Yes," I said. "It's both. I need to be able to tell his wife something."

"Because she blames you . . ." She nodded. "Makes sense. You *would* be the one to ask about such a cult."

"It's part of my process. I'm not about to join a cult and . . . and . . ."

"Masturbate with other men? Or maybe you're just scared of intimacy with anyone."

It was one of her favorite accusations. *Fear of intimacy,* she'd said like a diagnosis. *Explains what's happened in your marriage. Why Catherine left you.*

"Sorry," she said. "I get testy when I'm hungry. There is truth to it, though, isn't there? You have to work through those issues. Maybe you *should* schedule an appointment."

"I don't need an appointment," I said with much more emphasis than necessary. "I need a little help. Please give me something I can tell my friend's wife. Please, Marcia."

"Dr. Howler," she said. "Let's keep it formal. I see what's happening. She pressured you, or scared you, into helping and all you want to do is satisfy whatever you perceive as your obligation and wash your hands of it. Sound right?"

I wanted to challenge her, but she was right. At least she hadn't made a joke about what I'd rather be doing with my hands.

"Yes."

"Good," she said. "I'm sure your friend is in no danger, there are much more harmful sexual appetites than self-pleasure, but I'll help you."

"Thank you."

She gained more height and searched her pocketbook, found a capless pen and a business card, and wrote on it, using her long wallet as a flat surface. "My guess is your friend went to this man, a name I gave him, for research, and he provided information that led your friend to whatever cult it is he's joined."

"What's special about this guy?"

"He owns a unique shop."

"Sex store?"

"Antiques."

I waited for more but she offered nothing.

"Great. Thanks."

She did not offer the card. "He won't speak to the wife."

"What?"

An uncertain gesture, close to a shrug. "He has issues with women."

Was that yet another thinly veiled accusation against me?

"Meaning . . ."

She gave me the card. "Your obligation isn't over yet."

FOUR

THE NAME WRITTEN ON THE business card was Huey Marche. Beneath it, an address.

My stomach was grumbling, so I stopped at the Lexus Diner. It's on 9W near Route 84 outside of Marlboro. The address Dr. Let's-Keep-It-Formal Howler had given me was about thirty minutes south headed toward New York City.

I sat at the counter, ordered a bacon cheeseburger deluxe, and ate it slowly, cow-like.

The waitress kept refilling my coffee and asking if I needed anything else but I was lost in my own thoughts.

Why was I doing this?

Drew was my friend but we weren't overly close.

It's your fault, Elizabeth said.

Was I really that afraid of Elizabeth?

A little bit, yes.

It's your fault.

But that wasn't true. I hadn't told him to join a masturbation cult. I would've talked him out of such an insane thing if he'd mentioned it.

Except I hadn't even called him back.

Too busy doing you-know-what?

How's the masturbation addiction?

It's your fault.

The last I'd seen and spoken with Drew was that beer-and-scotch drinking session, but he'd left me a voicemail a few days ago. Why hadn't I told Elizabeth?

The voicemail was still on my phone.

Drew's recorded voice in my ear: "Hey, Mike, wanted to thank you. I'm onto something. It's big, *big.* Seriously. The book, oh, man, is gonna be, yes it is, something *special.*"

But none of that was actionable, as they say. Nothing in that voicemail provided any hint he was going to leave his family and run off with some cult.

Then why didn't you delete it? Or call him back?

Or at least tell Elizabeth about it?

It's your fault.

"Bullshit," I said. The waitress glanced at me but I waved off her concern.

This wasn't my fault.

What I should've done was finished my lunch, called Elizabeth to tell her what I'd learned, and let her go back to the police. They could handle it. They'd know how to interrogate Huey Marche better than I could. My obligation was over.

We writers are great rationalizers.

Why don't you have sex with Catherine? Dr. Howler asked during one of our couple's sessions.

It's not her, I said. *Sex is distracting. What I do is part of my writing process.*

Catherine hiccupped a laugh. *The great literary pervert,* she said. *One book and he thinks he's God's gift.*

Why can't you be happy for me? I asked.

She glowered. *Why can't you be* intimate *with me instead of with your hand?*

I put down the burger. I felt ill.

That night with Drew, he'd been hyper and self-interrupting so frequently—almost every other word—it should've been a comedy routine. Drew was always vacillating between quiet and near unresponsive—his default mode—and loud and overeager, a live power line whipping and sparking on the ground, when he was enthused.

I preferred him quiet, I guess. How else was I to be the focus of the conversation?

He was not quiet that night—he talked and talked and talked. It was irritating and upsetting, almost frightening. Or maybe that's me rationalizing again.

On and on, he spewed about his yet-to-be-written carnal masterpiece.

He didn't ask for help, didn't inquire about the sex therapist. He hadn't asked for anything, actually, but I'd given him her number. We were drinking, so that was part of it, but I'd also wanted to shut him up.

You're going to find him. Find him and bring him back.

I thought of Drew's video, the way his attention was super-focused for once, the way he was steadily touching himself the whole time, the way his pupils blacked out his eyes.

Drugs *had* to be involved. And if they weren't, what then?

"What the hell is going on, Drew?"

Whatever it was, I was not going to rationalize away my responsibility. Not this time.

I had to help.

Had to be an actual friend for once.

I took the food to go.

FIVE

THE ADDRESS FOR HUEY MARCHE, I figured, would be a sex shop or some seedy place where men in ball caps and sunglasses slunk surreptitiously in and out.

Instead, I was parked outside a roadside antique shop.

Just as Dr. Howler had said.

Blades of sunlight sliced through the clouds to reflect off the two other cars parked out front where an enormous wooden spool and an old rocking horse with gold leaf peeling off its face stood like sentries.

A hand-carved sign read: ANTIQUES and CURIOSITIES.

I called Elizabeth.

"Well?"

"I have a lead," I said.

"Good for you."

"I'm keeping you updated."

"What I need you to do, Mike, is find my husband and bring him back to me."

"I'm trying."

"You need encouragement, that it?"

"Fine. I won't call until I have him."

I expected her to hang up or curse at me and then hang up, but she breathed static into my ear and made a strangled, hitching noise that meant she was about to start sobbing.

"When you find him," she said in a barely-keeping-it-together voice, "you tell him that Wes wants to know why Daddy ran away."

Then she hung up.

~

A small bell jangled over my head when I pushed the door open and entered the antique shop. The store was quaint and cramped. Old-style big bulb Christmas lights sagged from the ceiling like the web of a giant spider. Shelves stuffed with artifacts jutted from the walls. A tall rack reaching to the ceiling showcased men's and women's hats, fedoras, panamas, church hats bedecked with ribbons, a funeral hat with a black veil. Furniture was wedged wherever there was space: here a mahogany wardrobe big enough for several people to hide inside; there a hutch with engraved hearts along the border; here one of those old desks where the top was on hinges and the legs carefully chiseled into something curvaceous and bizarrely sensual.

Or maybe I was reading into things.

The place smelled of old basements and mildew, but there was a sweetness wafting underneath, a thing I could almost taste.

There was a guy here who would lead me to a masturbation cult?

A middle-aged woman was looking through a box of black-and-white photographs. Next to that box was one filled with old keys.

She glanced up and nodded at me.

I nodded back and, to some people, that's considered an invitation.

"Hello," she said. She was cloaked in a blazer over a blouse. "Have you heard the good news?"

"Excuse me?"

"The Lord is risen," she said. She wore a gold cross on a necklace. Crumbly wrinkle-lines cut through her makeup across her forehead.

"Good to know," I said.

"Do you have God in your heart?"

"Does He need my permission?"

Her brow squished and her makeup crumpled. "You must accept Him into your heart."

"Maybe later," I said.

"What if there is no later?" she asked.

19

I'm not an anti-religious person, per se. I don't really care what people want to believe or how they want to practice those beliefs, so long as whatever they do doesn't hurt others and they don't try to force their beliefs on me.

But, ah, therein lies the rub.

How can a true believer resist the compulsion to share that belief?

I glanced around. Where was Huey Marche?

"You have a great day," I said.

The woman dropped the picture she was holding and moved much faster than I'd guessed her capable, snagging me by the wrist.

"I get a sense about people," she said. "God wants me to help you."

"You can take your hand off my wrist," I said as casually as I could. "That would help."

She didn't falter, didn't remove her hand, either.

"If you were walking down the street and you saw a house on fire and a person screaming for help from a top-floor window, would you simply shrug away their fate?"

"I'd call 9-1-1."

"That's what I'm doing," she said. "You're in a burning building. I'm calling God's emergency hotline."

Had she not been so damned insistent, so steady and intense in her stare, I would've burst out laughing. She really believed God was moving her to save me right now at this very moment.

"Maybe this can wait," I said. "I'm on a tight schedule."

"And when I call up to the man in the burning building and say I'm here to help, does he tell me it's okay, it can wait?"

"Look, I don't have time for this."

"You don't have time to save your soul?" She clucked her tongue.

"My soul's fine."

"No," she said, shaking her head. "It's not. I can tell. God is telling me."

She squeezed my wrist just enough to bother me.

"Thanks, but no thanks."

"You're lonely," she said.

"How astute."

"And sad. Your wife left you, didn't she?" The woman closed her eyes a moment. "She did. She left you because you didn't make space for her. You're an arrogant man, aren't you?"

"You must be a big hit at parties," I said.

She leaned in, pulling my hand toward her. "You must humble yourself before God. Give unto Him, and He will bless you many times over."

"Acquiesce, huh? That's all He wants? Absolute obeisance?"

Those forehead lines creased harder.

Now I leaned toward her. "You know, to accede, to comply, to supplicate, to kowtow, to cower, to lie down and roll over, to boot-lick . . . to bend over and *take it in the ass.*"

Her hand withdrew from my wrist so violently she almost knocked herself in the face.

"You're mean," she said. "You're *awful.*"

I finally laughed. "Yeah," I said. "That's what happens when you're trapped in a burning building."

She backed up and touched her cross.

"Don't worry," I said and grinned. "I'm not a vampire."

~

I walked to the back and found an old man sitting on a high stool reading a book. He was behind a dusty glass counter filled with old jewelry.

"If you're the owner, I must apologize. I think I offended one of your customers."

He spied me over the top of the paperback. It was an old, yellowing book, a scantily clad woman floating in outer space on the cover. He leaned to the side to peer past me.

The bell made its sound as the woman left.

"She's here all the time. Thinks she can save me."

"I guess we're both in a burning building."

He raised his other hand. Except there was no hand. Where one should be there was a fleshy stump, but I gathered he was raising it like a giant finger, telling me to wait a moment. He read another line or two, grinned, and lowered the book. Shadows nestled over his sunken eyes.

"Are you Huey Marche?"

"Eventually," he said in a musing tone, "someone is going to ask that question and not be a friend. Are you a friend?" His was the voice of an old man—strained and craggy yet higher pitched, as if old age reverted him back to his puberty days when words hiccupped between sonorous rumble and warbling squeak.

"I'm not here to cause trouble, if that's what you mean."

"Then, hello, friend," he said. "I'm Huey. Looking for something

21

in particular? Something risqué?" He flapped the book cover as if the woman on it were actually for sale, maybe stashed in the back.

"Dr. Marcia Howler sent me."

"I don't like doctors," he said, sounding bitter. "Especially female doctors."

He has issues with women, Howler said.

"She's a sex therapist. She gave me your name."

"Can't say I ever needed something like that." The old man was trying repeatedly to swallow, his throat making phlegmy choking hitches. Eventually, he succeeded and his gaze slid around the store and came back to me as he leaned close. "This isn't one of those pervy shops," he said, "but I do have some items of interest I could show you."

"I'm looking for my friend, Drew Delrose. Tall guy, nearly bald, can seem either aloof or totally wired."

"I'm getting lost here, young man. Have mercy on the old."

I chuckled good-naturedly. "Sorry. My friend Drew was working on a book and he went to Dr. Howler for research and Dr. Howler led him here to you, Huey."

"Ahhh," he said, dragging it out. "Makes sense now. Thank you."

"So, was he here?"

Yet again, struggling to swallow.

"You okay?"

He slapped the paperback down and coughed hard. Something wet splatted on the counter next to his stump. It looked like he'd hacked up a fleshy glob of his own throat.

"I think I can help," he said, his voice a thin whisper. "Wait right there."

The old guy turned slowly and shuffle-stumbled into a narrow doorway behind him.

He was nervous. I'd put a scare into him without even intending to. But he was going to give me answers. Had I thought the police better equipped to interrogate this guy? Shit, call me Detective Stiffe. (Remember: that's pronounced *Sty-fee*.)

A light came on, illuminating a small back room.

Huey Marche stood in the doorway, partially shadowed, one-handed and momentarily half-faced, and turned left.

Revealing a wall of shelves.

On those shelves: a Buddha with a very pronounced erection, candles in dented tins, what looked like a concrete dildo, and dozens of chubby cherub figurines that were also visibly aroused. Some of those phalluses protruded several inches.

Dr. Howler had not steered me wrong.

The old man emerged holding a large but slender book. I almost mistook it for a photo album. But when he set it on the counter between us, I saw it was the kind of book you imagine a monk might've made. You can see him sitting in a castle chamber hour after hour after day after month carefully hand scribing calligraphic letters.

"Too small to be the Bible," I said.

He grinned. "More than one bible. Christian. Jewish. Muslim. Mormon. Satanic. And many others."

On the cover, in bas relief so you can touch it and feel it if you so chose, was of course an erect penis.

"Sex manual?"

Huey opened the book. Pages crinkled.

"The Book of Onan," he said.

"Never heard of it," I said.

"It was Hebrew custom for a man to marry his brother's wife if that brother should die. Onan is told to do exactly that but when he fucks her he spills his spunk on the ground instead of inside her. It's okay to screw her, I guess, but coming in her is a step too far." He laughed and almost suffered a coughing fit. "God's so angry he *slays* him."

"That sounds completely insane," I said. "But it fits right in with a talking snake in the Garden of Eden."

The old guy chuckled but it crackled into a mucus-choked cough. I leaned back in case he hacked out another gelatinous glob.

"For the Hebrews, it was about tribal inheritance and a husband's obligation. For the Catholics, that story's all about not using birth control. Coitus interruptus is a sin. Every sperm is sacred." He managed a coughless chuckle, strained and phlegmy. "This book tells us the truth."

"It's a whole book about that one moment?"

"There are many, many lost books of the Bible. Forgotten books of Eden. The Book of Lilith. The Book of Noah. The true story of the Virgin Mary. Tales of Jesus the infant. The Gospel According to Pontius Pilate." He laid his one and only wrinkled hand on the open page. "The story of Onan, whom God slew."

"What *is* the story?" I asked.

The writer me was suddenly curious. How do you take a passage from the Bible that might be all of fifty words and expand it into a hundred or so pages? Tons of back story? Graphic depiction of the sex that so enraged God? How would I write the story?

"It's as grand a story as the fall of Lucifer or the resurrection of Christ Almighty," he said.

"I'm all ears."

He started to say something and the coughs hit again, doubling him over the counter, sounding so harsh and painful my eyes watered in sympathy.

No globs of anything spat out, but a single line of sweat slithered within his jawline wrinkles and he sucked at the air for several seconds before he could speak again.

"I got the cancer," he said. His eyes were rheumy, one of them bloodshot like Elizabeth's had been.

"I'm sorry."

"Read somewhere that if you live long enough everyone gets cancer. That's the bitch of it. But I ain't old as I seem. How old you think I am?"

"Sounds like a trap question," I said.

"Sixty-one. Believe that?"

"Lung cancer?"

"Throat," he said, the word sounding like a nail pulled from a warped board.

"That's awful."

"You're looking for your friend. How badly you want to find him?"

"He has a kid," I said. "An eight-year-old who misses his daddy."

Huey nodded and turned the crinkly pages of the book. Phalluses were drawn on many pages, text carefully stenciled around them.

"I know what you want to do," he said. "But you shouldn't do it. Your friend's gone. You go after him, you might be gone too."

"It's a masturbation cult, isn't it?"

"It's not about jerking off," he said. "Not the way you're thinking. It's about power. It's about worship."

"I promised to find him."

"You consider yourself a masturbator?"

He asked it so directly, I blurted my response: "Yes."

"How often?"

"I don't know."

He smiled to himself in a sad way. "I'm only prying because I need

24

to know if you'll be okay."

"Whaddya mean?"

"How often?"

"Often," I said. "What does it—"

"How's it make you feel?"

"Feel? Isn't that obvious?"

He shook his head, impatient. "Not what I mean. Some men do it and are filled with shame. Some do it and are filled with power. Are you shame or are you power?"

"Power," I said, though that wasn't entirely true. I typically did it because I was bored and lost, be that with my writing or life in general. So, "listless" might have been a better option. "Power," I repeated.

He thought about that. "If you don't take the oath, you may be okay. Your friend, though, he's taken the oath. Too late for him."

"What oath? What do you know about what happened to my friend?"

"What I know," he said, "is there are consequences for anyone who takes the oath, worships, and fails to complete the devotion."

"What does that mean? You try to leave and they hunt you down?"

He straightened and stared over my shoulder as if seeing something far off.

"'And when Onan was dead, his soul was cast into Hell with the other sinners. There did the Devil make a proposal of fortune and prosperity to Onan, which he took up eagerly. The Devil gave unto Onan special province of man's power. Any man who takes up his hand and his manhood thus pledges devotion unto Onan.'"

"Onan is the god of masturbation," I said. "Hence the word 'onanism.'"

"'He that worships fully and completely before Onan shall enjoy the exploits of divine revelation. Yet he that rescinds or relinquishes his fealty shall be punished tenfold in this world and in the next.' So reads The Book of Onan."

"Look," I said, "I don't care what the book says. I don't care what these weirdo masturbators think they're doing, worshipping some god or whatever. I only want to find my friend and try to talk some sense into him."

"I was one of the Disciples of Onan, the sacred worshippers. But I failed to complete the ultimate act of devotion."

"Which was?"

"Better you do not know," he said. "But my failure brought my punishment." His hand shook as it reached up to settle around his throat. He was still staring far off.

"The cancer?"

"What scares me is what's waiting for me *after* the cancer."

He thwapped his stump on the counter as if punching it.

"They cut off your hand? I don't believe that."

One unwieldy eyebrow lifted. "Imagine if they'd taken both."

"You're messing with me."

"Be hard to pray with no hands, if you know what I mean."

Maybe the cops *were* needed. They could tell him to take this culty nonsense and shove it. Cancer as punishment? A severed hand? Cut the shit, old man. Where's Drew? You better tell us, pops, or we'll arrest you for refusing to aid a police officer or worse, obstruction of justice.

"If anyone asks, I won't mention you," I said.

His gaze finally swam back to me. "I'm the only one who *can* help you."

"Will you?"

He sucked at the air and let it out through his nose. "Saint Agnes Hotel," he said. "It's just over the border in Jersey. Take this book." He slid it toward me. "It's your entrance ticket."

I glanced at it and he slapped the cover shut.

"Do *not* read it." He caught my wrist and squeezed. "The words have *power*."

"Sure. Okay."

"You'll have to prove yourself before they admit you. But remember: do *not* take the oath."

"Blood offering or something?"

"Or something."

I hesitated, my chest tight, mouth cottony.

"Should I be concerned or are you trying to scare me?"

"Both," he said and started coughing again.

SIX

CURIOSITY WAS BOUND TO GET the better of me.

I pulled into a rest stop that was asphalt and port-a-potties.

We've all seen the horror movies where the craggy old man warns the rambunctious and horny teenagers to stay away from wherever, and the other ones featuring a different set of idiot kids who discover the *Necronomicon* with a bloody note stuck to it warning anyone to not open it.

But of course they will open it. If they don't sneak into the abandoned asylum or read at least a little of the forbidden book, we don't have a story.

The old guy had freaked me out a little bit, the arm stump coupled with his nasty coughs got under my skin, but what he'd given me was not some book of the dead—it was for a stupid masturbation cult.

Stupid though it may be, shouldn't I know what I was getting myself into?

Your friend's gone. You go after him, you might be gone too.

Said the old man who was afraid he got throat cancer for failing to appease some bullshit god.

The burger was cold and the fries were droopy but I ate it anyway.

And I read.

I'd been right to wonder how a few lines from the "real" Bible could be expanded into almost 150 pages.

Well, you make the semen-spilling scene a ten-page dive into the minutia of sexual intercourse and the inner workings of Onan's moral conundrum. He's expected to impregnate his brother's wife and the offspring will be seen as his brother's heirs who will then inherit associated tribal rights and status, but Onan understands those children will actually be his and yet he will have no lineage connection. It's all in service to honoring his brother, the eldest male, whose death is no reason why he shouldn't have a legacy.

Anyway, Onan says to hell with that and pulls out and ejaculates on the floor. I don't know if the Christian Bible gives any detail about how exactly Onan is killed, but in The Book of Onan it is an angel of God who appears almost immediately, Onan still naked and dripping the last of himself on the floor.

This angel is horrifying. Onan falls to his knees. The angel declares that Onan has violated God's sacred covenant and pronounces judgment: Onan is to die and die painfully.

He does not beg for mercy.

Instead, Onan reasons with the angel, explaining from his standpoint it is unfair that should he have a child with his brother's wife that offspring will be his brother's lineage and not his own. Any child he conceives with his brother's wife would in fact have more rights than he himself.

The angel, of course, doesn't give a shit.

"You are unfavorable before the Lord," the angel declares. "He hath sent me hence to administer His judgment."

At that moment, Onan suffers pain like "dozens of blades stabbing his loins" and screams and cries. Yet even in his pain, he feels himself growing erect. He becomes larger and harder than he has ever known and within moments he empties his semen again—only this time it is blood that spills onto the floor.

It does not stop.

For failing to fulfill his responsibility to his brother's wife, Onan dies bleeding out from his dick.

No wonder that's not in the Christian Bible.

So, this story of Onan and his death, I imagined a pair of editors discussing, *kinda graphic, don'tcha think?*

Yeah, let's just change it to "And God slew him."

At that point, I'd finished what I was going to of the leftover food.

Onan is cast into Hell. The Devil applauds him and offers him the following choice: "I will raise you up to be a god among men, or you can suffer the indignities of Hell."

Apparently, many sinners in Hell choose to be punished because they "so fear the Lord and wish to make penance in hope for absolution."

Not Onan.

He says make me a god and the Devil does.

"Whenever man takes himself in hand," the Devil pronounces, "you shall be the one he worships."

Onan rises out of Hell to abide in the "ether of gods" from where he can see all who faithfully worship him, be they closeted or in the open field.

As I read of Onan the god of masturbation, I felt myself getting hard. *Really* hard.

I can't quite explain why. The book didn't turn into an erotic porn tale, not that I recall. And that's the thing—I wasn't sure *what* I was reading but I kept going. It was as if I were fluently reading a foreign language but without any comprehension of what the words meant. Does that make sense?

Either way, my erection was harder than I'd experienced in a long time.

Holy Viagra, I thought.

At some point, I was stroking myself through my pants and then yanking myself out into the open. Wouldn't take long. I'd been about to do this earlier when Elizabeth interrupted, so now it was a bit like unkinking a loaded firehose.

I was very close when I recalled Huey's words.

Do not read it. The words have power.

The words, I thought. *The words are getting me hard.*

I saw Onan falling to his knees before the terrifying angel and I heard him scream in pain as he ejaculated streams of blood that would not cease until he was dead.

That should've killed any arousal but it didn't. I was so hard and my hand kept stroking. *It's like I'm possessed,* I thought. Faster and faster and—

I grabbed a handful of used, greasy napkins to catch my semen.

You are unfavorable before the Lord!

But I wasn't coming. I stroked faster and faster. My dick burned.

THE HANDS OF ONAN

I couldn't stop. Faster and faster and faster.

The semen bulged inside me but it wouldn't break the seal.

"Fuck!" I screamed.

And punched myself in the face.

My head knocked sideways—and the crazed masturbation trance was broken.

Someone knocked on the driver's side window and I screamed again.

A child of eight or nine stood there on the other side of the glass waving at me.

"Get away!" I shouted.

The kid was yanked backwards, his smile dissolving into surprised fear, and then a tall man stared down at me, his jacket pulling tight across broad shoulders.

"Sorry," I said, "I didn't mean—"

The man opened the car door, which I'd failed to lock after using the port-a-potty, and hauled me out by my neck. I stumbled and tried to pull up my pants. The man grunted something derogatory and punched me in the gut. My intestines squished into my throat. I crumpled.

"Goddamn sicko," the man said.

Thankfully, he didn't kick me when I was down.

SEVEN

WAITING FOR THE THROBBING IN my gut to ease, I sat in my car and called my friend Marshall. He was a painter, favoring large canvases, some as big as the side of a barn. His schedule was not predictable, so it was a 50-50 shot calling him. But I had a question for him, and he and I were of a similar ilk, you might say, when it came to process.

Marshall was a masturbator.

"Hey," he answered.

"Hey," I said and cut right to it. "I found something that's ... Well, it's troubling but maybe also extraordinary?" I'd shut The Book of Onan and pushed it into the passenger footwell. I stared at it as if afraid it might open like a mouth and attack me.

A dog barked on Marshall's side and another answered. A moment later, a chorus of barks made it sound like he was at a pet shelter. Marshall was a fellow divorced forty-something, had no wife or kids. Unlike me, who hadn't tried to fill the void with anything but my own manhood, he'd filled the empty spaces in his life with canines.

"Bad time?" I asked.

"No, no," he said and whistled to his dogs. The barking stopped, mostly. "They're excited today. There's going to be puppies."

"You're going to have more dogs?"

"You could take one."

"I doubt I'd be a good owner. Last pet I had was a goldfish named Spike that died when I overfed it."

"A dog is not a goldfish. A dog would be good for you. It will awaken something inside you didn't know you needed."

"You writing self-help columns now?"

Another chorus of barks and another whistle to quiet them.

"What is it you want, Mike?"

"You still masturbate?"

He chuckled. "That's why you called? To ask if I jerk off?"

"Humor me."

He started to respond, paused. "You mean when I'm painting?"

"Yeah."

"Occasionally, but not much anymore. All the dogs keep me honest. Weird to do it when they sit around watching."

"So what do you do when you feel the urge?"

"It's like alcohol," he said. "I just don't take a drink. I get back to work."

"Right," I said, though it felt like he'd insulted me somehow.

"That's what you wanted to know?"

I was staring at the penis on the cover of The Book of Onan.

The words have power.

I felt the compulsion to grab the book and—

"Earth to Mike. Hello?"

"Sorry, yeah, I'm here." I had to force myself to stare out the driver's side window, but I felt the book as if it were a person staring at me. "When you're painting and really in it—"

"In the House of All," he said, which was how he thought of that special state of hypnotic flow that happened sometimes when he was working and everything that wasn't the act of creation fell away.

"Yeah, when you're in the House of All, how do you break out of it?"

"I wish I knew," he said, "and then I wouldn't let it happen."

"Right, but is there something that typically breaks the spell?"

"Exhaustion," he said.

"You ever fall into the House of All and you want to get back out?"

"What exactly is the issue?"

"Okay, I have this book that when you read it, it puts you in a trance-like state."

"Self-induced hypnosis. Cool."

"Not really." I hesitated. "You end up jerking off without meaning to."

"Whoa, a masturbation hypnosis book."

"Literary Viagra," I said.

"Why would you want to break that spell?"

Because if you don't, you might never stop jerking off, I thought.

"Humor me," I said.

"Hit yourself?"

"I did."

Now that the pain in my gut was easing, the soreness in my face took over. I'd given myself a pretty good punch.

He chuckled. "Wait—you're serious?"

"Yeah. This isn't some story idea I'm writing. This is real. And the book is a religious text or something. An alternate Gospel or whatever. I think there's a whole cult built around it."

"What have you gotten yourself into?"

"I don't want to hit myself again," I said. "Any advice?"

"Don't read the book."

"I won't."

Except, my worry was bigger than that. What if someone read the words to me? What if a congregation recited the words and it induced a mass hypnotic state?

"What if I have no choice?"

If I'd called someone who wasn't a creative, someone who didn't paint or write or even dance, my question would've elicited disbelief. You always have a choice, such a person would say. We creatives know that isn't always true. When the story takes us, when the canvas demands paint, when the stage cries out for movement, we must answer or a piece of us dies.

"The act of creation," Marshall said, "is a balance between ego and humility. If you're too humble the art won't be brought forth from the ether of wherever it exists. Too arrogant and the art will refuse to be your servant. But if I were already in the House of All, I could end up trapped there if I gave myself to it, if I was too humble. So, if I wanted to get out, I'd have to tip the balance the other way. Embrace the ego."

"How?"

THE HANDS OF ONAN

The dogs were barking again.

"Don't know. Paint my name really big?"

He whistled but the dogs kept barking.

"Look," he said, "whatever it is you're caught up in, don't be an idiot. I'll call you later."

EIGHT

I GOT BACK ON THE ROAD.

Next stop: Saint Agnes Hotel.

Don't be an idiot.

Too late for that, Catherine would say.

I kept glancing at the book in the footwell, as if expecting it would open on its own. Could it actually be a magical text? That was ridiculous, and yet how else could I explain what happened to me?

The words have power.

I'd experienced it first-hand, you might say.

I thought of Drew's enlarged pupils, of the way he spoke in a calm-yet-wired way, and how he stroked himself as if his erection were separate from his body.

I have to do this, he said. *There's magic here.*

There is no sex. Masturbation is not sex. This is so much more powerful.

Another glance at the book.

"I should burn it," I said. "Pull over and burn it right on the side of the highway. What do you think of that?"

The book did not respond.

I couldn't burn it, of course. Huey said it was my entrance ticket.

THE HANDS OF ONAN

Do not take the oath, he warned.

"I'm going to save Drew," I said. "That is exactly what I'm going to do."

My voice sounded more confident than I felt.

NINE

IF A ROADSIDE ANTIQUE SHOP can house a back room replete with phalluses along with an ancient book written to honor the god of masturbation that gets you hard just by reading it, what sort of depraved curiosities might be hidden in the closets of the Saint Agnes Hotel?

Unlike your typical Ramada Inn or even HoJo's, the Saint Agnes Hotel was not a commercialized building with a garish sign and sliding glass doors.

It might've been one of the innumerable old hotels you can still find in Manhattan, the building narrow and quaint, the lobby small and off which a cocktail lounge, lit in dim red, promises the illicit libations of an age long lost to history.

And here it was on a New Jersey back street as if transported whole and dropped from some other time and place.

I started to call Elizabeth and stopped. *What I need you to do, Mike, is find my husband and bring him back to me.* I texted her instead: *Saint Agnes Hotel. Drew may be here.* And I added the address.

"Can I help you, sir?"

The man behind the dark wood reception desk was giving me the obligatory smile, both obsequious and impatient. He wore a sleek black suit with a red bowtie.

I hurried toward him as if moving fast would prevent him from noticing my sneakers, jeans, and tee shirt, but he was a master of the up-and-down judgmental appraisal.

"Checking in?" A single eyebrow lifted toward his slick hair.

"No, I— Well, I have *this*."

I held up The Book of Onan, the Braille-like erected penis on the cover.

"One moment, please," he said and used the old-fashioned candlestick phone on the desk to make a call so brief I missed what he might've said.

"Margot will be with you momentarily," he said to me.

Masturbating Momentarily with Margot, I thought and wondered if I was losing it.

Even when I turned my back and stepped away from the desk, I felt the man's stare between my shoulder blades.

A door opened somewhere in a dark recess and a woman click-clacked on high heels out of the shadows. She wore a perfectly tailored business suit, a red silk scarf slipped along her throat matching the lipstick standing out against her pale skin and mascaraed eyes.

"Hello," she said. "I'm Margot. Welcome."

Although she was almost excessively polite and also alluring (intentional or not), I felt as unsure as I'd been a moment ago with bowtie guy at reception.

"I'm Mike."

She waited.

"Stiffe. Mike Stiffe," I said.

"Welcome, Mr. Stiffe." *Sty-fee*.

"I have this book."

Gently, she took it from me, glanced at it, traced a hand down that penis, and looked back at me. Had she noticed how I shook when her fingernails slid down the cover? Her expression wasn't one of lust or desire, not even flirtation, yet it was one that teased such unsaid and unpromised things.

Maybe I only thought that because I'm a writer.

Or because she was a beautiful woman and I'm depraved. Or pathetic.

"I see why they have you here," I said and grinned like an idiot.

"Follow me," she said.

We went into the shadows.

The hotel lobby glowed behind me in a rusty light as if it were a distant place far away, and until she opened a door, the woman was a darker shadow inside a bigger one. I could, however, feel her there. Without sounding too much like a toxic male, I can say that for a moment she was pure physical impulse and I could've reached out and grabbed her.

But I'm not *that* guy.

Yet my point is the same: If there was a masturbation cult somewhere in this hotel, it made perfect sense for this beautiful woman to be the gatekeeper.

The men could fantasize about being her key master, and that would help them put things in hand, as it were.

Something unlatched and a door opened to a stairwell only slightly better lit.

I followed the clack of her heels down two flights.

"Can I ask you something?"

She did not respond.

"I'm looking for my friend."

"Good luck with that," she said.

"I guess what I'm asking is . . . what am I about to get into?"

She paused mid-step but did not turn to look at me. "I've never been beyond the threshold."

"What does that mean?"

"It means, men do whatever men do and I'm just as happy to stay out of it."

She went the rest of the way down to a sub-basement level. The floor was concrete, the air cutting with a chill.

A single red bulb lit a black door.

Several feet from the door, she stopped and gestured toward it.

"Do I knock?"

"They're expecting you," she said.

"And the book?" I asked.

"I'll see that it's returned to Mr. Marche," she said.

"So he can give it to someone else?"

"That's the way it works."

I hesitated. Gone from her face was any trace of flirtation (if it'd ever been there at all). This was a trap, right? Had to be. What I should have done is gotten the hell out of there, called Elizabeth, and . . . And what? Called the police? *There's a masturbation cult in the bowels of*

THE HANDS OF ONAN

that hotel!

She gestured to the door.

"No clue what I can expect?" I asked.

"They're going to take your clothes." She said it in a cold, mocking voice, as if she'd known what I'd been thinking about her as the male masturbation fantasy and wanted to make it clear I was the one about to be taken advantage of, not her.

She headed up the stairs, the darkness folding around her.

I stood there until the clack of her heels was the sound of my heartbeat in my ears.

This was another horror movie moment. *Don't investigate that strange sound you heard. Don't go in the basement. Don't pretend there's nothing to fear.*

Except there wasn't a killer on the loose. No ghosts. No demons.

Was I really afraid of a bunch of men jerking off?

I knocked.

TEN

BEFORE THINGS GOT REALLY STRANGE, I was able to keep my bearings enough, as they say, to be fairly confident in what I'm relaying here. Everything so far—from Elizabeth to Dr. Howler to Huey Marche to Margot—was exactly how things transpired. Once I entered the room in this sub-basement of the Saint Agnes Hotel, however, my recollection of events cannot be completely trusted. Part of it was the heavy darkness weighing everything down, and part of it was the masturbation.

It's difficult to testify with any sort of veracity when you've been stroking yourself for what could be hours.

It makes memory an unreliable bastard.

~

The door opened.

A skinny sallow-faced man stood not two feet away. He wore what looked like a black graduation gown. If I hadn't been so startled, I might've asked where his mortar board was.

"Come in," he said, his voice a scratch of rock against stone. Maybe he had throat cancer too. At least he had two hands.

He shut the door behind me, and we were in complete darkness.

THE HANDS OF ONAN

The room was warm, quiet. I sensed other rooms nearby, could even hear faint sounds like talking or singing.

"Strip," the man said.

"No," I said.

"Then you can leave."

I felt him reach past me to the door.

I sensed someone else in the room, a shadow person, a watcher.

"I'm here to find my friend. That's all I want."

"No one gets past this room without a cleansing."

"A cleansing?"

"Strip."

"Then what?"

"Then we'll begin the cleansing."

"I showered this morning."

"Not that kind of cleansing."

"I'm not taking an oath."

The man made a strange humming-gargle sound.

"You hear me? No oath."

"Strip."

So I stripped, all the way. I told myself that if I felt in danger, I could punch this guy out, assuming I could see him, and then run the hell out of here. A voice in my head asked if I thought fleeing up the stairwell butt naked was a feasible escape plan, but that didn't stop me from pulling down my boxers.

What almost stopped me was my phone and my car keys. They were in my jeans. I should take my phone out and use the flashlight to see who else was in this room.

"Here," the man said.

I reached out, afraid of what I might touch, and felt a cheap imitation silky fabric, some acrylic blend of synthetic materials. My own personal graduation gown.

I put it on and bent down to get my phone and keys, but the clothes were gone.

"Where are my clothes?"

"You'll get them back," the man said.

Someone was moving quickly along the far side of the room. A blade of blue light severed the darkness, expanded, a man's silhouette stepped into it, and the blue light vanished behind a closed door.

Mr. Shadow Man had made off with my clothes.

"What the fuck is going on?"

"If you wish to proceed any further," the man said in that gravelly voice, "you must do what I say and be open and honest. I will know if you're lying."

"I thought this was a masturbation cult, not a therapy session."

"It's the greatest therapy known to man," he said. "Walk forward five steps, stop, and sit cross-legged."

I did.

The room was not completely dark, and my eyes were beginning to adjust to it. The man's face was so pale it seemed to radiate light.

He sat a few feet away, facing me.

Were we going to meditate?

"Your first orgasm," he said.

"What?"

"Your spermarche," he said. "Describe how it happened."

"I was eleven and had a wet dream."

"No," he said. "The *details*."

"Okay," I said. "I was eleven and there was this girl, Kelly—"

"First," he said cutting me off, "we must breathe."

"Thought I was."

"Breathe in slowly through your nose, a count of four. One, two, three, four. Hold the breath for the same count, and release slowly out your mouth, counting to four again."

"I'm not here for yoga or meditation," I said.

"It's part of the cleansing."

"And so is telling you about the first time I ejaculated?"

"It's the source of all your trauma."

"Now you're a therapist?"

"In The Book of Onan, it says, 'Unburden thy self from the shame of hand and member and embrace thy godliness.'"

"Well, that explains everything."

"Breathe in," he said.

I did. I breathed in slowly, counting cartoon numbers in my head that floated up and away, held my breath, and breathed out.

This was stupid, but I'd already come this far and Drew was down here somewhere. A little breathing, a slightly embarrassing story about my first wet dream, and then I could find my friend and drag him away from these weirdos.

Assuming I could find my clothes and my keys.

I smelled something like incense yet sweeter.

It's a hallucinogenic. They're drugging me.

THE HANDS OF ONAN

The sudden panic stopped my breathing.
My pale-faced friend stopped as well.
"What's that smell?"
"We must start again," he said. "*Breathe.*"
In, hold, and out. Slowly.
My head got lighter. My body relaxed.
I'm getting high.
Yeah, from whatever they're pumping into this room.
Maybe, but it felt good.
I was as relaxed as if I'd emptied my balls.
"Now," the man said softly. "Your first orgasm."
"I was eleven . . ."

ELEVEN

I WAS ELEVEN AND HAD, from time to time, started noticing little things—Kelly Munk's large blue eyes when I could get her to look at me in class and how sometimes her shirts were too big and a bare shoulder was naked in the neck hole, or the way the high school girls who ran track glistened with sweat when they were done sprinting and sprawled themselves on the field near our playground, their bodies heaving breathlessly.

The dream is as clear to me now as it was vivid for me then. There I am, eleven years old, sitting at my desk in class but no one else is there. A pencil sharpener is on my desk, one of those old metal hand-crank ones, and I'm sharpening this one pencil but it's not working. The blades grind away and I turn the crank again and again. Something about the motion feels right—one hand gripping the pencil, the other working the crank. "That's how you do it," a girl's voice says, so light and pretty. And there's Kelly Munk right next to me except she's older, like those track girls, and she's breathing like them too, chest filling the space between us, her breath on my face, and she smells of sweat and Juicy Fruit gum. "Let me help you," she whispers. One hand of hers covers the hand I'm holding the pencil with, her other hand covers mine on the crank. I quiver like I'm cold but it's a good kind of cold. She leans so close her lips are at my ear. She says something but I don't hear it. There's a puff of air into my ear and I wake. My pillow is beneath me and I'm humping it in crazed, frantic jack-rabbit thrusts. It's the greatest feeling I've ever experienced. I could do this forever. But then there's this other sensation I've never known. An intense pressure building inside me. It feels like my guts are filled with lava. I'm suddenly scared. Am I sick? Going to puke? Shit myself? But I can't stop thrusting, it feels so wonderful. The bed springs are making loud sproinking noises. The lava-pressure builds and builds and when it erupts I am sure I am going to die. I'm burning up. My every muscle is tense. My testicles are so hard and jammed up against me. My penis, though, my penis is a solid steel pole. If it gets any harder it's going to rupture. Then it does rupture. Something is coming out of my penis. It *hurts*. My dick feels like a piece of wood that's spitting splinters. I can't breathe. This is not right. Something is very, very wrong with me. I am definitely going to die. It's only a few seconds but feels like forever. When it's over, and I'm panting, I expect to find blood smeared on my sheets but the whitish gunk on my pillow, sheets, and Batman pajama bottoms is so bizarre I glare at it uncomprehendingly in the glow of my eggshell nightlight. What is this stuff? Something *must* be wrong with me. An infection or a disease. I'm scared and embarrassed. I've got to clean this up. I make it only a few steps into the hall before Mom appears in her bedroom doorway. The rooms share a wall. She must've heard me. My shame is magnified a millionfold. I begin to cry. Mom thinks I've had a nightmare and all my insistence that she doesn't need to put me back to bed only makes her more adamant to do so. And when she sees the sheets she says, "Oh. Well. It's better than wetting the bed the way you used to."

TWELVE

ALL OF THAT—THE STORY, I mean—spilled (*ejaculated?*) out of me in an insistent rush. I didn't consciously choose the details or make any decisions about what to say. I just said it.

And now I was even more relaxed. I could almost trick myself into thinking I was lounging in a warm bath.

"Here is my story," the man said. His voice was extra low but strained, as if he'd been screaming, and as he spoke it was as if I inhaled his words with my steady breaths. "I watched my father die. Happened in the kitchen. We'd had dinner—Cornish hen, mashed potatoes, green beans—and I was upstairs in my bedroom all ready for bed but doing math homework. Multiplication tables. I was in fourth grade, a good student, and a good kid too. I knew enough to stay out of my parents' business. When I heard the first sounds, I ignored them."

I could guess where this was headed. Literally, thousands of people have seen their parents have sex and it always starts with hearing strange noises and feeling compelled to investigate.

Most horror scenarios begin the same way.

"Sounded like they were moving things around. Chairs scraping.

47

Plates and forks and knives. Mom laughed, but it sounded different. That's what made me leave the math work on my bed and tiptoe into the hall to the top of the stairs."

The light was changing, not getting lighter exactly, yet I could see the man a bit better. He was so skinny as to be emaciated. His skin was tight beneath his eyes and across his cheekbones. A quivery energy was coming from him, like he might grab me and yell in my face.

"By the time I was coming down the stairs, my parents were grunting and moaning, not super loud but loud enough. There was another sound too, a really familiar one.

"Those sounds made me stop on the stairs but it's not what you're thinking. It didn't sound like they were fighting or wrestling. It sounded the way the cafeteria did at school—everyone gobbling food in open-mouthed chews and slurping milk and juice in liquidy sucks.

"For whatever reason, I thought they were having an eating contest. I was a kid, so that idea seemed possible."

"Mom was on her back on the table and Dad was standing over her. His shirt was off, big belly hanging there, and Mom's legs were bare and up on his shoulders. Her jeans and underwear were on the floor. Dad's pants were puddled around one leg. He was fucking her, obviously, and also obviously this was the first time I'd seen such a thing. He was thrusting, whole table shaking. They hadn't even cleared the table, so the dirty plates were still there with the forks and knives clattering and Dad's beer had spilled in a puddle and the inch of milk left in my glass was shaking. I tried to focus on that. It was like that movie where the T-Rex shows up, you know, the concentric circles vibrating in that cup of water. My whole body went cold and I couldn't move. My father grunted louder and louder.

"There was also a box of Drake's Coffee Cakes on the table. It was my father's go-to breakfast, snack, and dessert. So, he's grunting—getting close—and Mom's moaning, holding onto the table as everything's shaking on it, and Dad snatches a package of coffee cakes out of the box. There's two in a sleeve, wrapped in plastic. Dad shoves the end of it into his mouth and squeezes the bag so it pops and then he's chomping on a coffee cake. Crumbs fall all over. They're falling on my naked mother as he's thrusting away and I can't move, can't look away.

"He gobbles one coffee cake and then the other. He's chewing this one when he finally opens his eyes and sees me."

Why I needed to hear this story I wasn't sure, but I felt surprisingly relaxed. My breathing continued that same deliberate way—in, hold, out.

And I could see vividly everything this man was describing, the inch of milk shaking in the glass, the coffee cake crumbs cascading onto bare flesh, as if I were inside his memory and standing right behind his fourth-grade self.

"He sees me and something melts hot inside my chest," the man said. "Feels like one of my organs is bleeding out. Still, though, I can't move.

"Dad grins at me. He actually grins. Coffee cake crumbs speckle his cheeks and chin. He doesn't stop fucking my mom; in fact, he thrusts fast as he can. He's watching me with this goddamn grin as he finishes. His fat belly seizes up like a boulder and Mom's crying out. They might've just had the best sex of their lives.

"And then Dad's grin sags and his eyes go big but it's like they're not focusing. He jerks back from the table, stumbling, almost tripping. He's making this strange throaty spluttering noise.

"Dad's hands come up as if reaching for his throat but they don't make it there. They flutter at his shoulders. His face speckles with crimson blotches. Eyes so wide I really thought they might fall out. His nostrils get big too. I see that perfectly, the way they flare. Like he was trying to inhale some smell. He stumbles side to side and it reminds me of when I saw him and Mom dancing at Uncle Mike's wedding.

"His eyes are tearing and his hands try for his throat again but they thwack against his chest. The sound is so much like the fleshy noises they were just making. He's groping at his chest like he's trying to pull something out of it.

"Mom is up on her elbows and saying his name over and over— *Rob? Rob? Oh, God, are you okay? Rob?*— and then she's getting off the table, my milk tips over, a plate clatters on the floor where it wobbles like a giant coin, and I have a full view of my mother, completely naked. Her back is splotched red and mashed potatoes are wedged in her ass crack. When she moves behind my father, I see her entire front. I am completely ashamed and embarrassed, but I can't look away, can't even close my eyes, and they're burning because I haven't blinked. I *have* to watch. There is no other option.

"She's behind him, smacking his back, hitting hard, battering palm-punches. His eyes are even wider, but they roll up to an all-white that makes me think of maggots squirming in roadkill. He's making thick, hollow, phlegmy hacking sounds. Brownish drool dribbles off his lips. He's shitting out of his mouth, I think, but of course it's brown because of the coffee cake.

"Mom tries to get her arms around Dad's chest. He's choking and she's going to do the Heimlich thing they do on TV, but her arms are too short and his chest is too wide. Except she *could* do it but she's coming from around his arms instead of under them.

"I see that error clearly. I'm a little kid but I can see she's doing it wrong. I try to scream, to speak, to point—something, *anything*—but I just stand there watching.

"Doesn't matter. It's almost over."

The man took a breath and chuckled. It sounded like old newspapers crumpling.

"He didn't last very long after that. Crazy how quickly it happens. He did another weird slow-dance shuffle and collapsed. He hit the table on the way down and his weight should've tipped the damn thing but the table stayed upright and my father's head caught the angled corner and he hit the floor hard—a dull, heavy *thunk*. From where I stood, I saw his head. He was facing me. His eyes rolled back to normal but there was nothing in them. No life. Blood spread in a puddle from where his head hit the table. Mom looked so shocked but also accusatory, like it was my fault. She didn't even try to cover herself."

He paused long enough for me to think the story was over. I was drifting, my whole body unhinging and turning wobbly.

"Then Mom saw: I'd ejaculated in my pjs. I hadn't even realized. While watching my parents fuck and my father die, I'd had the very first orgasm of my life."

I tried to speak—*Jesus*—but my throat was too dry to make a sound and my lips felt glued together.

"Before The Hands of Onan rescued me," the man said, "I suffered a long, long time."

My head was swimming as if I'd been drinking.

The darkness was changing again, swirling, gaining and losing texture.

I heard chanting coming from just beyond this room.

"Here's a perfect example: I was in line at a grocery checkout," he said. "Only had a few things. I don't eat much. I'm behind this couple. Twenty-somethings. They can't keep their hands off each other. Kissing and hugging. It's obnoxious. They're buying snack food. Probably stoned on something. Spending their day doing drugs and fucking. Worked up an appetite. Chips and cookies and a big plastic jug of cheese balls and a package of Hot Pockets and"—he paused, and I knew what he was going to say—"a box of Drake's Coffee Cakes.

"So, there I am waiting in line watching these two lovebirds grope each other and then you know what they did? She grabs the Drake's, rips it open, tears open a plastic pouch and shoves one in his mouth as he goes to kiss her. Crumbs and pieces and chunks tumble all over. They're laughing and still pawing at each other, ready to tear each other's shirts and jeans off.

"I'm watching this and I'm hard as a goddamn steel pipe. I'm going to shoot off in my pants. I take it out, start whacking right there. The girl sees and screams, the guy spits the Drake's all over the place, and the cashier runs toward the Customer Service desk, shouting for the manager. Everybody is watching. I keep going, and I grab the other coffee cake and shove it in my mouth. Just as I'm coming, I vomit. It drenches my shirt, splatters all over my sneakers. Then I run outside and vomit in the parking lot. When I got home, I jerked off and puked again.

"That was my life for years. Until Onan rescued me."

I still couldn't speak and, honestly, what the hell could I say to that story?

"You shared your first orgasm," he said, "but what is *your* enduring trauma?"

THIRTEEN

TRAUMA?

I'd had a wet dream and my mother saw my spunk on the bed. Probably happens to damn near every boy. I certainly didn't feel compelled to whack off anytime I saw Drake's Coffee Cakes.

Men jerk off. It's what we do.

Except . . .

How's the masturbation addiction?

I almost called Catherine, but the last thing she'd want is to talk about you and sex. She said you wouldn't fuck her anymore. All you did was masturbate.

"Tell me," the man said again. "What is your trauma?"

I didn't think I could speak, but I opened my mouth and the words were there.

FOURTEEN

I GOT MY FIRST SHORT story published when I was fifteen. It was entitled "Pledging My Love" and was published in a fanzine that paid in black-and-white photocopies of the mag. I didn't care. It was amazing. I was an actual published author. My mother told all her friends and all her friends' friends. When one of them suggested my mom host a party and have me read the story aloud for everyone, however, my mother politely demurred.

It's a wonderful story, she said, *so imaginative. It's just not everyone's taste.*

Remember Kelly Munk's blue eyes and bare shoulder? By the time I was fifteen it seemed every girl was less than the sum of her parts—eyes, shoulders, lips, legs, butts, and breasts. That's all I wanted, and it consumed my mind. Didn't matter what any girl wore, even the most loose-fitting, shapeless, baggy sweatshirt became a fixation for curiosity and fantasy-building. What was under that sweatshirt? How soft was the skin? I walked through school some days with my book bag in my hands to hide an almost relentless erection.

Some school days I'd get home so overwhelmed with all the images (real and imagined) of every girl's lick of lip, curve of breast, scoop of butt, sway of hip, and flex of thigh that I'd barely make it into my room before yanking out my dick and jerking off with a ferocity that's both ridiculous and humbling.

Every day was a buffet of female bodies, but there was one girl who became my, well, my obsession. Move over Kelly Munk—hello, Rachel Linkly. Dark hair, glasses, always raising one slender arm in class with her fingers curling as if around an invisible lightbulb, skinny, hair in a ponytail, and clad always in tight clothes that looked painted on.

In tenth grade history, we were assigned to the same year-long cooperative group. Ms. Urbin believed in what is now called "constructivist pedagogy." Essentially, figure it out for yourselves, kids. Misguided teaching method or not, group work let me stare at Rachel for at least a half hour every day. She was kind too, smiling at me, and she would touch my hand when she thought I was losing focus. I pretended to lose focus frequently, and when she touched me it felt like her fingertips were charged with electricity. The sensation quivered on my skin for hours.

This is how obsessions are born.

Lucky for me, and lucky for Rachel, I was a writer. We writer types seldom take any real-world action. We're shadow people, lurking along the perimeter and documenting and imagining and fantasizing.

I'd been writing stories every so often for a few years. Some were pretty good, most were awful though fun retreads of favorite movies, *Terminator* and *Total Recall*. But one day, I sat down at the Brotherhood Word Processor, which my parents had given me as a birthday present when I turned thirteen, and I wrote what would become my obsessed-with-Rachel story, "Pledging My Love."

The story is simple: A pimply, fat adolescent grows obsessed with a gorgeous blonde cheerleader, who then publicly rejects him, so he kidnaps her, ties her to a tree, sexually assaults her, and sets her on fire. The story's final line is something like "Her eyeballs melted down her face like the tears she should've shed for breaking his heart."

Melodramatic and yet there's truth there too, I think.

My mother read the story, eyes growing wide at certain parts, lips gently patting together at other parts, and when she finished she took her time aligning the pages of my story before smiling at me and saying she thought it was very good, a bit violent, but good. And then she asked if the poor doomed cheerleader was based on an actual girl.

I felt Rachel's electric touch on my flesh. "It's just a story, Mom."

She wasn't completely satisfied with that answer because, although I was skinny and had decent skin, it was pretty obvious the pimply fat kid was me.

Dad read it, declared it "Not bad," and asked if I was pining for a particular girl.

"No, Dad. It's just a story."

He didn't believe me, either.

But one day he came home and handed me a book: *The Writer's Market*. In it, I found listings for magazines and fanzines seeking short story submissions. I followed the instructions, typed up a cover letter, and mailed my story out (including a self-addressed stamped envelope) to four magazines.

One never responded. One came back with a Return to Sender stamp on it. One rejected it in a terse two-line letter typed on a sliver of paper: *Too graphic. Not for us*. And the last one called my story a "profound (and profoundly sick) tale of obsession" and declared they would publish it and for which I'd be paid in "ten contributor's copies."

Those contributor's copies were photocopies stapled together, but I was a published author at fifteen years old. Look out world, Mike Stiffe is coming!

Pun very much intended, except that was the problem.

Numerous times during the writing of that 18-page story (almost 4,000 words!), I dropped my pants and stroked until I came. Almost used half a box of tissues.

Maybe my writing was turning me on—"the ropes pulled tight across her body so her breasts were even larger than normal, engorged and inviting"—but thinking about it now, it seems obvious that it was the masturbation itself, and it was the beginning of my problem.

I was obsessed with jerking off.

Two, three, four times every day.

The urge would take me and it got so I couldn't resist. I'd run off to a bathroom. Or if I were in my bedroom, I'd drop my pants and have at it.

One time, there were no tissues on my nightstand and I didn't have time to grab a sock or shirt from my dresser, so I grabbed the nearest thing: a stuffed animal left over from when I was five or six. A Care Bear. Sunshine Bear, to be exact, bright yellow and smiley with a faded sun on its belly.

I came all over Sunshine Bear's face.

Instead of throwing it out, I stashed it under my bed.

Several more times, I used Sunshine Bear as my personal sperm catcher. There must be a website devoted to Care Bear sexual fetishes, but I'm too afraid to check.

The face was crusted over, cloudy like thick ice, and each time I grabbed the stuffed animal, white flakes fell off it like dandruff.

Then one day the Care Bear was gone.

My mother found it while vacuuming and threw it out. She didn't say anything about it, but the look in her eyes when she mentioned running the vacuum through my room was a mix of judgment and concern I'd see again years later when Catherine, my wife, found me whacking off . . .

"Be honest," my wife said to me, "would you rather masturbate than have sex with me?"

When we were having sex, I'd imagine I was actually masturbating. I fantasized about pleasuring myself in order to get off.

Dr. Howler suspected as much, I think, and may have said it to Catherine.

Doesn't matter. Point is: masturbating destroyed my marriage.

Maybe I should be the poster child for "masturbation is sin" and travel the country giving speeches to horny Catholic girls and boys.

How's the masturbation addiction?

Depends, do you think of breathing as an addiction?

FIFTEEN

"THERE'S MORE," HE SAID. "WHAT is it?"

"The story that ended my marriage," I said.

"What story?"

The story was titled "The Sins of Louanna and Ray." It was a riff on the American-tourists-travel-to-a-foreign-land-and-end-up-in-hell horror trope. It was a sex story and meant to be creepy and could easily be titled "White Fear in Foreign Lands."

It's a pretty good story, I think, but it also reeks of my own desperation.

Doesn't matter anyway.

She never read the story.

SIXTEEN

The Sins of Louanna and Ray
by Michael Stiffe.
(Never published.)

SHE SAID HE'D GET USED to the heat, but four days here and he's still a soggy dishrag of sweat after only a short walk through what passes for the town. He's in shorts and sandals and a short sleeve button-down like any other white guy on a tropical vacation, but she's in tight jeans and a turtleneck, which is insane. The day is hot, yes, but it's the humidity that's the problem. You can squeeze fists of water out of the air. Dressed as she is, she should be drenched and overheating. Instead, she's upbeat and perfectly comfortable.

Louanna is also twenty-two and Ray is, well, considerably older.

They were chased off the beach by scrawny snarling dogs, so now they're in town and Ray follows Louanna into the fish market tent.

Machetes chomp and rattle, cutting up the morning's haul, and ungloved hands wrap the chunks in newspaper for customers. An elderly woman with only three teeth slaps the pink-and-white slabs as if spanking a child. The stink infects the whole place in a dense cloud.

"Should we get something?" Louanna asks.

"Why?"

"Because we're here."

The old woman is watching them. Her right eye is squinting and a fat green fly crawls along a wrinkled groove in her cheek.

She hefts a fat fish on the table before her, spank-slaps it, and readies the machete.

Louanna is walking around as if browsing in some clothing store.

In the distance, thunder crackles. The daily afternoon storm. The pale blue sky will darken to lumpy black, thunder will rip open the clouds and for a minute or two heavy rain will fall. Then the clouds will slide away and the sun and the humidity will return, often stronger than before.

Thunk.

The fish's head wobbles to the edge of the table and falls off into a bucket overflowing with guts.

Chomp-rattle, and the fish is quickly cut in thirds.

They should be back at the hotel, not mixing among the natives. Stay out here long enough and you'll start calling yourself Kurtz from *Heart of Darkness,* and you won't be lucky enough to end up fat and worshipped like Brando in that old Vietnam War film.

No, you'll end up spanked and chopped in thirds.

"Are you laughing because you're scared?" Louanna asks. "Or because you're a fascist white pig?"

"Let's go with the second one."

"I want coffee," Louanna says. "Something hot."

His mouth is too sour and raw to respond. A sip of coffee would make him pass out. Might be what she has in mind. She could leave him in one of the plastic chairs outside the fish market tent. He'd wake, dehydrated and punch-drunk, his wallet and sandals stolen, fat green flies buzzing around him, and he'd try in vain to find his way back to the hotel. He has a terrible sense of direction, doesn't speak the native tongue—doesn't speak anything other than English—but the street people would know where he was headed and could help. *If* they wanted.

He doesn't like being out here. It's not only the heat. He feels exposed. Vulnerable.

"Let's go back to the hotel."

There is only one place on the island where Americans (and similar-minded Europeans) ever go. It is the only reason for visiting this place. You don't come here for the homeless people sleeping along the dirt ditches where spoiled food sloshes in piss. You aren't here to get bowel disease or to return to the states with some bizarre worm parasite a doctor has to remove from under your flesh to then keep in formaldehyde for testing.

You are here for the hotel and its promises.

Back in the street, two emaciated men, arms long and sinewy, whistle at them as they pass. One man thrusts two fingers inside his fisted hand and the guy next to him unhinges his jaw to unleash a long, flicking tongue.

The street is almost empty but Ray has a distinct sense of an unseen multitude. As if people are hiding inside these ramshackle buildings and peering out from whatever shade they can find.

Louanna spins around and slips up against Ray so her small breasts push against him and her bony hips collide with his. Four days here and he's already lost five pounds. She's always been skinny but soon she'll be skeletal.

He's getting aroused.

She feels it too and her face calcifies, eyes dark and judgmental.

"Would you do it right here?" she asks. "With everyone watching. Bend me over and fuck me?"

She moves her hips and a small groan quivers in his throat.

The men are whistling again.

"Come on. *Do it.*"

His hands stretch over her butt, as small and tight as a teenager's, which she practically is.

"It'll take ten minutes to peel off your jeans."

"Time for a crowd to gather."

His lips are sandpaper. The day is now even warmer and his skin feels tight, the pores clogged, all the sweat stopped up inside him.

She presses harder, the crease of his fly against him is painful in a way that makes him squirm. She digs in with her hips. The whistling gets louder, cheering her on.

"Don't play dumb," he says through his teeth. If she keeps going, those whistlers are going to watch a forty-year-old man come in his shorts.

A twenty-two year old girl will do that to you.

"I don't play anything," she says, lips at his chin.

She moves those bony hips and grinds her crotch as if she wants him to bleed. It wouldn't surprise him.

"Suck me off," he says, trying to sound commanding.

60

"That's against the rules."

He's squeezing her ass as hard as he can. Under the jeans, it's probably going red and purply.

Through his shorts, the hard denim of her jeans strokes him like a brick wall against a bare hand and the pain is successive, lightning-white flashes of wonderful pleasure.

God damn this girl.

Thank God for this place.

"Let's go back," he says.

"But I want coffee."

"There's coffee at the hotel. You drink the swill they sell out here you'll get diphtheria."

"You mean dysentery."

"Whatever."

Her face as set as stone, she grinds against him hard enough to earn an "Ow." Her expression doesn't change. It never changes; even when he manages to make her come hard, the most she's ever given him is a lip bite betraying her pleasure. What of it? He doesn't need her facial expressions.

He needs only her body.

He goes to kiss her, not because it's what she wants or even what he wants (what he really wants is to strip naked and lie on the hotel bed with the A/C and the ceiling fan chilling his body), but because he has to do something, he can't keep looking at her statue-face while he throbs against her crotch, but she smears three fingers across his lips and presses them into his teeth.

"Ow," he says again, this pain worse somehow than the hurt in his groin. He'll make her pay later.

He'll make her obey him.

Or she'll make him obey her.

She pushes him back and when he tries for her arm the whistling guys call out to him. He has no idea what they're saying but it makes him feel more exposed and even more overheated. They're pointing and laughing, mocking him.

One of the fish sellers emerges from the tent. It's not the old woman but one in her thirties or forties with broad shoulders and long dreadlocks. She does, however, have a machete, three feet long.

She taps it against one thick brown thigh. She sees him staring and grins around extra-large teeth. A car horn blurts and someone else shouts what must be a curse word. A boy of ten in jean cut-offs is pedaling his bike slowly past. Something is rusty and squeaks repeatedly. A teenager with jutting buckteeth pushing back slippery lips, splays Polaroids from both hands like fans or a magician doing a trick. The pictures are a smear of pale flesh in erotic positions. The camera, straight out of the '80s, hangs around his neck.

The street is now abustle and the sense he had earlier of unseen multitudes returns with the strong fear he should not be out here. They should've stayed at the hotel. Louanna wanted to "take in the local flavor," but really it'd been because the bartender at the hotel had been talking about the "weird local customs." He'd even used the word "ritual" and suggested, as a brave American couple, Ray and Louanna might enjoy a "jaunt among the savages." Ray did not like the look in the bartender's eyes, but Louanna stood up right away and declared that was exactly what they were going to do.

Only someone so young could be so brave.

Or stupid.

More thunder. Getting closer.

"Let's go back," he says.

But she's already a hundred feet farther down the road. Her head swivels side to side, checking each store front and dilapidated shack beneath a crooked tin roof.

"Hey," he says. "*Hey!*"

The whistlers turn it up loud and the machete woman makes a deep throaty sound like a whale call. This gets the whistlers laughing. The kid on the bike has stopped and is shaking his head. The Polaroid man raises his pictures overhead and thrusts his hips. The kid on the bike then makes that same fingers-thrusting-in-a-fist gesture one of the whistlers made.

Across the street, a girl of maybe fourteen or fifteen (though she could be as old as eighteen, it's so hard to tell) is giggling in a polka dot dress, red barrettes in her black hair. Ray saw her earlier when they left the hotel. She was leaning against a post talking to one of the guards who carried AR-15s slung across their chests. Now she's next to an older woman taking a long drag on a cigarette before flicking the butt into the street.

Had the barrette girl followed them?

"*Hey,*" he tries to yell but Louanna is too far now and his voice too brittle.

She's talking to a shirtless guy in a blue porkpie hat. He gestures for her to come inside and she doesn't even glance back down the road before disappearing into some shack with a peeling-paint front and a mangy dog outside licking its balls.

"*Louanna!*" he shouts.

The world goes mute—or he's now deaf. Either-or, it's the same. Sound has died. All is silence.

The men keep laughing. The woman works her mouth around whale sounds he can no longer hear. She looks like she's calling out across a far distance. The kid on the bike tugs something from the pocket of his shorts. It's a paring knife. He clenches it in his mouth like a pirate. A little girl waves an armless doll back and forth overhead like a signal. The barrette girl stands straighter. The woman next to her lips a new smoke but does not light it.

Ray is more scared than before, a lot more, but he can't quite explain why. The silence is part of it but there's something else.

He's done something wrong.

Yeah, yeah, you have—coming here. Cheating on your wife.

No, this is about the *rules*. He's committed a transgression.

They're all staring at him, frozen-stiff mannequins, and he knows he should run but he can't find the strength or muster the will, nor would he know which way to go.

Never leaving the hotel should've been Rule #1—follow that and just about anything goes. Bondage and sodomy, even bestiality, for God's sake. Not that he would ever try that.

He learned about this little island and its hotel from some of the older guys at the Chowder Club. Sears, who was sixty-something, did most of the telling and his eyes sparked a youthful glint when he freely shared his three-day sex adventure here.

But the place has rules, Sears said.

What rules? Ray asked.

No names. There's power in names. Power enough to awaken the gods of blood and death.

Ray dismissed that last part. These old guys were always trying to freak him out with stories about haunted houses and demon possession and whatever else they could think up.

Sure, sure, Ray said. *Everything anonymous.*

Sears grinned. *Follow the rules and you'll be safe.*

The concierge explained more rules when they arrived two days ago, and though he heard them, he also struggled to keep his eyes off Louanna's slender feet in high-heels. He developed a whole fantasy about them and by the time they made it to the room, Ray was hard as a steel pipe, harder than he'd been since his teenage years when chasing cooze was second only to getting drunk and high.

No names, the concierge said. *Not for the next three days. That's rule number one.* He was a small man with small hands he kept folded on the desk before him. His shirt collar was so tight it pinched his flesh. *No sex outside the hotel is rule number two. Again, only for the next three days. No cellphones, of course. Not ever. No email. No computers.*

He went on and on but Ray was off in his foot-job fantasy.

Whale-sound woman is raising the machete, blade rusted and dented but the slicing edge shiny silver sharp.

Fear squeezes his heart and lungs together, but she isn't attacking, she's waving, gesturing, signaling.

Down the road where life is as still and silent as here, two men in Hawaiian shirts wave back. One has a pistol in his hand, slinking hunched over, and he disappears into the shitty little place Louanna went into.

He'd said her name.

No names. Not for the next three days.

Christ, he thought they meant stay anonymous. They literally meant *no names.*

"What are you going to do?" he asks no one in particular, but it doesn't matter anyway because he can't hear his own voice.

The boy on the bike punches fingers into fist. He's laughing, as are the whistlers and now the others who've come out to crowd the street. The old woman is out too, her own machete serving as a cane, and Mr. Porkpie Hat ducks into the coffee shop (or whatever it is) and emerges to lift his hands in two A-Okay gestures.

"I'm sorry I said her name. I wasn't thinking. *It was an accident! I didn't mean to transgress!*" He can't hear the words except as they sound in his head, and he hopes he doesn't sound as panicked as he feels.

Why is he so scared? He broke some stupid rule. Big deal. What're they going to do, kick him off the island? No way. They need his American money. His repeat business. What kind of stupid plan would kick customers off just for saying a name?

White fear. That's all this is. He's out among the natives and it's gotten to him. People don't like to admit it, but it's true—he's a wealthy white American and as such he's not used to being among so many dark and poor.

How is that his fault?

The two Hawaiian-shirt guys bring Louanna back down the road.

They each hold an arm and carry her so she bends her knees to save her feet. Her silver toenail polish glows in the sun like coins.

They are carrying her back for punishment—a flogging, a public humiliation—and her face is as unchanged as ever.

She must be scared, at least worried. She's just better at hiding it than he is.

Or she's accepted what's about to happen. Submitted. The way she accepted him as an older lover—with acquiescence and complicity yet also a degree of empowerment. She has what he wants—youthful sex—and she knows how to torture him with it.

A little public flogging might even be a turn-on.

The two men drop her to her knees but don't let go of her arms. A fly crawls along her right temple. She stares at Ray, unblinking.

The street is completely crammed with people. Where did they all come from?

Why are they all here right now?

What is about to happen?

Even if he knew the native tongue, there's no point in asking because he can't hear.

Hands grab him by the elbows and the waist and he's hoisted on shoulders like the player who makes the game-winning goal.

Louanna is lifted as well, except she's lain flat across a stretch of raised arms.

Like an offering, he thinks.

The crowd marches.

It's a procession.

More people join the crowd. They are chanting.

They're heading toward the beach. The sky is thick with storm clouds.

Stray dogs are running across the beach and fighting with each other.

He feels something wet on his skin. It's not raining yet.

They are splashing him with something. Oils. Hands slap at his body.

On the beach, they are dropped onto the sand.

She's dumped in front of him, both of them with the stretch of ocean beyond.

Maybe that's all this'll be. Carried out here and abandoned. Punishment.

Fuck me, Louanna says.

He still can't hear but he's sure it's what she said but how could that be right? Did the crowd march them here just to watch them screw?

A final humiliation?

No sex outside the hotel is rule number two.

What is going on?

Fuck me, she mouths again.

He nods.

The Hawaiian-shirt men lift her again, holding her with both hands so her feet dangle. The boy with the knife in his mouth hurries over, kicking up sand. He unbuttons her jeans, unzips the fly, and starts tugging them off her angular hips.

But as Ray predicted, it's as if the jeans are painted on and the harder the kid tugs the tighter the jeans cling to her flesh.

The old woman hobbles over, machete as a cane.

She's going to hack the jeans clean off except it won't be clean at all. It'll be a bloody mess of lacerated flesh—the chomp of blade against muscle and bone, and blood will splatter.

Not that he'll hear any of it, but his eyes will take in more than sight. Through vision alone, he'll absorb sound, smell, and touch—exactly as he does when Louanna sprawls naked on the bed and he tells her what to do as he watches from the corner.

The old woman points at Louanna's hips with the machete and the kid folds the top edge of the jeans down onto itself and proceeds to keep folding the denim into a thick roll that exposes skin inch by inch.

The boy's fingers snag the edge of her white panties and the tan line dipping between her hip bones makes Ray's blood jump. The boy does not remove the panties but continues peeling the jeans. Ray does not follow the roll of jeans down her thighs. He can't look away from that tan line. The way her underwear is pulled crooked, he wants to lick the flesh along the edge. Smell her sweetly pungent body sweat and touch her. She's not aroused, how could she be, but she's twenty-two and it won't take long.

The jeans are tugged off her bare feet, her sandals tossed aside. The boy bunches the jeans in his arms, looks at the old woman who nods, and scrambles back to his bike. He doesn't pedal away, of course. Wouldn't want to miss the show.

They want you to fuck me.

One of the men holding her up is getting visibly excited, tongue licking his lips and pants tightening.

Ray is getting aroused too, God help him.

He might be in one of the sex dreams he had almost nightly during adolescence—weird shit where he'd fuck girls who were pale blue and stuffed head-first in the frozen food bin at the grocery store or he'd seduce some girl with tears on her cheeks or (and he'd never admitted this to anyone) a guy would finger his ass while whispering Ray was a bad boy as girls pointed and laughed. Most nights he'd wake humping his pillow.

The middle-aged woman with the dreadlocks chews at the air, the humidity so thick she might really be eating it.

She faces Louanna.

The machete comes up fast—right to Louanna's throat—and stops. Her jaw rests on top of the blade. With her other hand, the dreadlock woman snatches Louanna's panties and yanks them below her sex.

Then those unwashed fish-gut stinking fingers grab Louanna and enter her.

Finally, Louanna's expression changes.

Her eyes peel huge and her mouth scoops wide.

Shock? Pain? Pleasure?

All three.

And, shit, Ray is so hard now he might shoot in his shorts. Talk about being a teen again.

He also wants to vomit. The back of his throat is acid.

The aroused guy holding one of Louanna's arms is now stroking himself through his pants. His tongue dangles like he's one of the dogs on the beach.

Louanna is shaking, eyes rolling to white.

Is she really getting off so quickly?

The real question is not how rapidly she's orgasming but how she can at all in this situation, but Ray doesn't consider this. He's getting close to getting off as well.

Someone is unbuttoning his shorts.

He stops himself from looking all the way down.

He sees the red barrettes.

The girl uses both hands to pull him out of his shorts. Her hands are on him.

No. This is wrong.

Terribly, terribly wrong.

But it must not be against the rules.

They want you to fuck me.

Those hands are working him so quickly he'll never make it to fuck Louanna. But she's in another full-body quiver. The woman is really giving it to her.

Ray wants to grab this girl who has her hands on him and red barrettes in her hair and yank up her polka dot dress and—

His orgasm is the most massive he's ever experienced. His entire body is servant to it. Not all orgasms are equal, as we all know, and this is one against which all future ones will be measured.

His mind blanks, his every muscle spasms, and he ejaculates in successive bursts that bulge from within and rocket through his erection with so much force his dick feels like it might erupt in a grenade explosion of blood, flesh, and semen.

His entire being is the come shooting out of him.

He is screaming—

—And sound fills the world again. *I can hear!* But what he hears is not his orgasm howl but the unholy, the unsanctified, the unrighteous cries of the gods the locals call the World Eaters.

It is not thunder, though it could be mistaken as such. It is an otherworldly, all-consuming god-howl.

Louanna is orgasming again. The guy next to her is ejaculating as well and, impossible as it is to believe, Ray is still shooting streams of spunk. It's like his entire body is filled with the stuff and his cock is a faucet turned completely open.

He is drenched in sweat, screaming, and crying too but doesn't realize it. Louanna is experiencing yet another orgasm and her pain is more than she can endure.

It's almost over.

The gods demand worship and the gods demand sacrifice.

Tourists never follow rules. Especially white American tourists.

But in the end, it's quick.

The locals are faithful servants, not sadists.

The women use the machetes to get it started. Ray watches a giant gash spread Louanna's chest in a bloody smear. The men holding her slap hands in the wound and use her blood as lubrication on themselves.

Ray, still orgasming, vomits.

The puke is thick grayish-red gruel.

The old woman stands before him. She says something in a language he doesn't understand. Truth be told, the woman doesn't understand it either. She knows only that it must be said.

It's how it's always been done.

She kisses his forehead. It's almost tender.

She steps back, lifts the machete—and swings.

After that, the locals use their hands like claws to strip flesh from bones. They collect the lungs, the heart, and the liver for later rituals. Of the rest, they eat what they want, slurping flesh and sinew, though they are not cannibals, and leave the remains on the beach for the dogs.

The rains will fall and the tide will come in and all will be washed clean.

~

Straight out of the Grindhouse features, circa 1960s and 70s, but considering how things turned out with the Onan cultists, it's more prescient than I'd like it to be.

~

I was writing the ending of that story when Catherine walked into my office and found me with one hand on the keyboard and another on my erection.

"Be honest," my wife said to me, "would you rather masturbate than have sex with me?"

I couldn't respond.

Not verbally anyway.

Instead, I turned back to the computer screen and the words written there and finished what I'd started.

She watched me from the doorway as I masturbated.

When I was done, she said, "You're the worst kind of man. All self-worship."

Within a week, she handed me divorce papers.

SEVENTEEN

"THANK YOU," THE MAN SAID. "You are cleansed. Now, you will discover the glory and the power of Onan."

I heard his voice, but it was muffled and distant. I was rising upward from the watery depths of sleep.

No, you're emerging from a drug-induced hallucinogenic trip.

"You do not need to be a slave to your sexual impulses. Onan will show you the way."

The room was no longer quite so dark. Maybe my eyes had adjusted. Or maybe there was some guy tucked away working a control board and watching me on a monitor. Bring up the lighting a bit, decrease the incense output, intensify the blue glow cutting out the rectangle of the door.

"You will transcend your conception of your sexual self," the man said. His waxy face floated before me. "The Christian god wants procreation, but Onan demands no such servitude."

My brain was a flexing sponge. I felt the soft squeezing sensation behind my eyes and down through my teeth.

"It has nothing to do with sex. Onan is all-man, and man is all cock."

A doodle-do, I thought and tittered like a little kid.

"You will be freed from your traumas. You will embrace the power that is uniquely yours. Welcome into the Hands of Onan."

The man stood, his movement so fluid it was jarring, and I wanted to look away because it was making me dizzy but my eyes tracked him as he slipped to the door and opened it for the blue world beyond to blaze across me like otherworldly fire.

EIGHTEEN

THE BLUE ROOM WAS AN anteroom that tunneled toward another room. Men stood along the sides of this passageway. They were each in a black cloak and humming a low electric vibration. My skin tingled as I passed each one.

At the next door, my pale-faced guide spoke with a large man who might've been functioning as a bouncer.

"By the Hands of Onan."

"By the Hands of Onan."

Then the door was opened to us, and I followed him.

I'm not sure what I expected, a bunch of men whacking off in zombie-like mediative states. *Jerkoff Zombies,* I could call them. Maybe a large statue of this Onan god, lit candles, more incense, and a preacher giving, shall we say, hands-on instruction?

Instead, the room might've been someone's furnished den. Wood-paneled walls. Dimly lit sconces. Leather wingback chairs. Only thing missing was a small bar and the smell of cigar smoke.

Perhaps fifteen or twenty men, each one in a black gown, stood around like a class of graduates killing time before the commencement ceremony.

My guide, Mr. Sickly Face, blended into the group.

This was where Drew recorded that video.

I looked around but could only turn my head slowly because of the dizziness. They'd definitely drugged me, hotboxing that other room with some hallucinogenic that made me share all that nonsense about masturbating and trauma, and that same truth-serum shit might be pumping in here.

I had to focus. Get my bearings.

Where was I?

You're in the subbasement of the Saint Agnes Hotel.

No, not where am I, but why *am I?*

Shit. So much for bearings.

Your clothes. Find your clothes. Get your phone and your keys and get the hell out of here.

Yes. That sounded like a plan. A thing on which to concentrate, anyway.

Someone touched my shoulder. I spun around too fast and stumbled a step or two like a drunk.

"Whoa," the man who touched me said. "You're okay."

The man's bald head shone as if polished.

My mind recognized him before I did, if that makes any sense.

"Drew?"

"Hey, Mike. You found me."

He was so damn normal about it, we might've been running into each other at the grocery store.

"Drew?" I said again.

"Yes, it's me." He flashed a salesman's grin.

Two things struck me immediately—Drew was more confident and focused than I'd ever known him to be and his face was almost as jaundiced as the other guy's had been, unhealthy yellow and sunken beneath the eyes and in the cheeks. His voice was strained too, as if from sickness or incessant screaming.

Of course, I was probably under the influence so I couldn't even trust my impression.

"Elizabeth sent me."

"I can't leave."

"Can't or don't want to?"

"You don't understand. I found something special here, truly."

"Bullshit."

"You shared your trauma, didn't you? We all have traumas. Onan

73

can free you from them."

"I don't have a trauma," I said. "I didn't have my first orgasm watching my father die, like that demented sicko, wherever the hell he went."

"It's all the same. We are all prisoners of bodies society has vilified."

"I don't even know what that means."

"Self-pleasure is the gateway to oneness with our god."

"You sound insane."

"There are men here who were heroin addicts who are now completely healed. Men who tried to kill themselves who now have a reason to live."

"Trade one addiction for another," I said.

"Don't you want to be a better writer? Onan can help. He'll give your words life they've never had before."

"Oh, really? Is that why your face is skinny as a concentration camp inmate's?"

"You don't need to eat much once you've given yourself to Onan. He will sustain you."

"Drew, you've been brainwashed. *Warped.* I'm going to get you help."

"I have been helped. I have purpose now. I've never seen so clearly before. I used to be so nervous. So anxious. It's all gone. Onan freed me from the prison of my trauma."

"This is a *cult!*" I spit the word, not caring if anyone else heard. I was suddenly pissed off. I was here to help him because his wife had guilted—even threatened—me into saving him from this warped cult and now I was here, naked beneath a black robe in a room full of men dressed the same, in some secret room beneath a hotel on a back street in New Jersey. "We're getting out of here."

"No," he said.

Drew's lips did a weird quiver that was almost a smile but made me think of someone about to have a seizure.

"You're not okay."

"I'm perfect." Spoken like a true disciple.

"Where are my clothes?"

"There's no reason to be afraid."

Around us, that electric-humming sound trembled softly, building louder and louder. The other men were doing it, as if there'd been a secret signal.

A hive mind, I thought. *Brainwashed.*

I grabbed Drew's arm. "We're getting out of here, *now.*"

He didn't move. He'd lost weight and was even skinnier than usual but he could've been made of concrete for all the good pulling on his arm did.

"It's okay, Mike. You're among friends."

The light caught his eyes then—his pupils were so large they blacked out his eyes and that blackness didn't even twitch in the spill of light.

"We are the Hands of Onan. You are one of us."

"Not me. Where's my clothes?"

The humming was suddenly much louder, as if I were standing inside a bee's hive.

"You're not going anywhere," Drew said.

I sensed the room closing in, but it was actually the men, all of them now encircling us and humming loudly and menacingly. Fear like hot liquid spilled inside my chest.

I wasn't inside a beehive. This was a wasp's nest.

"Drew, we have to get out of here—"

But now he was humming too.

NINETEEN

THE HUMMING GOT LOUDER AND louder and—

A tall man raised his hands before the group and the humming dipped to a low undercurrent of sound. It did not, however, stop, and it was like being able to hear electricity and that made me uneasy.

This was supposed to be a simple thing. Find Drew and bring him home to Elizabeth. Instead, I'd fallen under the spell of a masturbation gospel and now I was in the basement of a hotel with a bunch of black-cloaked men.

I'd convinced myself there was nothing to fear. This was a bunch of men who believed jerking off gave them power, not a satanic sect kidnapping and murdering virgins to a goat devil.

There weren't any weapons anywhere. No reason to be scared.

The words have power.

Do not take the oath.

I needed to grab Drew and get out of here.

Where were my clothes? My car keys?

"Drew," I said through my teeth, "let's go."

He ignored me. He was staring forward. Humming.

"Welcome, gentlemen," the tall man said. His voice was gravelly like the man's to whom I'd confessed my masturbation trauma. Robed like everyone else, he raised his arms like a priest blessing his congregation. His arms were startlingly pale. "You are here because you know now the essence of man. The ingredients of our power. A man's cock is his power."

The collective humming rose in an audible wave and smoothed out again.

"But that power is not simple biology," the man said. "We owe our special province of power to the god who gave it to us. But we must be dutiful. We must obey his demands. We must take up our hands and our manliness and genuflect in worship."

Another rising tide of humming.

The man was too far away and the room too dark to make out his face, but the light caught his eyes. They gleamed with the same sort of madness in Drew's. The same in everyone's here.

What about mine? Was I beginning to take on that same look?

"Onan demands worship," the man said. "We must humble ourselves before him. We must take the oath and abide his will. Only then will we know the glory of his blessings and the true power of ourselves."

"Drew," I said again. I grabbed his arm, tried to pull him. He was like stone.

"There are consequences," the man said, "to false worship."

A man near him, who I saw was Mr. Pale Faced Drake's Coffee Cakes, handed the tall man something.

He took it and held it high.

A human hand.

No joke. He was holding a severed hand by the wrist. It was an adult hand but frail and slight. The fingers were curled in a loose fist. The flesh looked gray.

It couldn't be real, though. Right? A fake hand, even a cheap one from a Halloween store, would look real in this poor light.

Except, it *was* real.

It was Huey Marche's.

I had no reason to believe that to be true, and it was impossible to tell from this distance, but I felt the truth of it just the same. These people really were insane—both deranged *and* dangerous.

I failed to complete the ultimate act of devotion, Marche told me.

Which was?

Better you do not know.

What could possibly be so terrible to do you'd rather get your hand cut off?

"All who enter into The Temple must pledge devotion. There are no exceptions. Onan demands it. Any who fails to give of himself fully and without ego to our god will be punished. Be it any of you, or even me. Disobey his will, and we must take a hand as offering. As recompense. As atonement. As penance." He paused, breathed out. "Any who pledges and then breaks his oath will lose all that makes him powerful. Be such a sinner, and we must take your manhood."

Manhood? Did he mean . . . ?

If these cultists were willing to sever hands, perhaps it wasn't much of a stretch to sever something else off a man.

"Let us go forth into The Temple and pledge ourselves unto *the Great Onan!*"

The humming was immediately loud, a giant wave of it crashing inside this room.

My hand was still on Drew's arm. I pinched it hard and yanked him toward me.

"*Now! Let's go now!*"

He turned to look at me. His humming was violent and electrical. He leaned toward me. His pupils were enormous.

I let go of him.

Being here was wrong. I should not have come. Or at the very least fled after texting Elizabeth this location. Let her save her husband.

More men turned to look at me.

Images from horror movies flickered through my mind: zombie hordes and demon-possessed attackers.

Run, I thought. *Just run.*

I tried.

TWENTY

EVEN IF I'D BEEN ABLE, it would've been pointless to resist.

I did scream a little and managed to shake off the first few hands that grabbed, but then there were many more hands, snagging my robe, seizing my arms, legs, and neck—and I suffered a panicked vision of them strapping me onto a rock slab and performing some ritualistic sacrifice.

They hurried me into yet another room.

The Worship Chamber.

I must've been high because when the men seized me it was like a many-handed monster lurching as one, raising me up in offering, and I felt my brain tilt back as if it had shrunk or my skull had enlarged and my brain was a jostling, spongy blob. My eyes wouldn't stop slipping around in their sockets so the lit candles in this new room smeared like bug guts across the windshield of my vision and I couldn't discern what enormous thing it was in the center of the room that emanated a moon-like glow until they forced me on my knees before it and declared it to be Onan the god himself—a giant glistening phallus.

I should've burst out laughing.

I should've gotten up and run the hell out of there.

I should never have gone looking for Drew.

Each man kneeled before the enormous cock. It was maybe fifteen or twenty feet tall and six or seven feet wide throughout from base to tip where a vertical crease divided the top into the familiar mushroom-like head.

A tall candle flickered between each man.

My stunned reflection gawked back at me in the gleaming slick of its hide.

The room was humid and smelled faintly of a summer rain.

Drew was next to me, still humming.

"Now what?" I asked. "We just start jerking off?"

The humming got louder and louder.

"They going to pass around a porno or something?"

Then the humming stopped all at once, and what rose into that silence were words of a tongue that was long ago dead, if it'd ever been spoken to begin with.

I couldn't make sense of what the men were now chanting and yet I knew: the language of Onan.

"Drew, this is fucking crazy. We need to get the fuck out of here."

Except I couldn't even get up from my knees.

His head swiveled to face me. The candle flame flickered between us.

"It's not crazy," he said in a terribly flat voice. "It's the answer."

His head swiveled back and he rejoined the chant.

I tried to stand and could not. My legs were completely numb. In fact, I couldn't feel anything from the waist down. Was I paralyzed? Had one of the men injected me with something when they carried me in here?

Then I realized something else.

My lips were moving.

I was chanting the words in synchronicity with the men.

I had no idea what the words meant, and I can't describe the discordant chop of consonants and smushed stretch of vowels, but they were flowing freely out of my mouth as if some part of me knew the words.

The phallus glowed brighter, flickered, dimmed, glowed even brighter yet.

I tried to keep my mouth closed, tried to tell my jaw to stop moving, my lips to stop parting, my throat to stop making noise, but I could not.

Next to me, Drew had tugged up his robe and was slowly stroking his erection.

All the other men were as well.

Chanting and stroking in unison.

I did not feel anything but sensed movement and, sure enough, my hand was busy doing what it'd long ago mastered. My erection was so thick and large I marveled at it.

I'm hallucinating. I have to be.

I better be.

The phallus dimmed and once again shone so brightly it was as if clouds parted for an enormous burning sun and shadows of the kneeling men cut into the walls.

I still couldn't feel what I was doing to myself, but an electric sort of energy now quivered through my chest. My heart felt twice its normal size, but instead of that being frightening it was empowering. I felt strong. The way a body builder might after lifting heavy weights, muscles engorged and convulsing for more weight.

If you don't take the oath, you may be okay. Your friend, though, he's taken the oath. Too late for him.

Shit. The oath.

Was I saying it right now?

I couldn't stop.

What else had Huey Marche said about the oath?

What I know, is there are consequences for anyone who takes the oath, worships, and fails to complete the devotion.

What the hell was the devotion? What was the consequence if I failed to take it? Cancer? A severed hand? I thought of his stump, fleshy and raw.

I kept going. All the men kept going.

It could've been minutes. It could've been hours.

Masturbating and chanting.

No wonder everyone's voice was fucked.

It was surprising their dicks didn't fall off.

The phallus burned bright as a white sun.

Something was inside it.

A large indistinct thing. It loomed in there. Hazed as if in fog but getting bigger, it could've been a giant man or a bear standing upright. Only bigger. *Much* bigger. It had heft. Closer and closer, and it took greater shape and as it did, it looked less and less like anything recognizable outside of a nightmare.

Hunched and hulking, it was a creature of magnitude and weight. Thickness and girth. It was close, whatever the hell it was, coming from some other place inside that phallus. Or the glowing dick was some dimensional portal. It should've been ridiculous enough to dismiss but real horror, real monsters, are only funny if you're not the one facing them. It was very close and *I was afraid*. I did not want it to get any closer. Didn't want it to emerge out of that glowing phallus. I was terrified what would happen if I saw it clearly—both to my mind and of what that *thing* might do to me.

You should be scared. You know what it is.

Onan.

One of the men, robed but with a drooping hood hiding his face, was walking around the circle. He was not masturbating, nor did he appear aroused. He was short and skinny enough that the robe made him look like a wraith. He circled the group and stopped behind the tall guy, the man I assumed was the leader, and set something on his shoulder.

The kneeling man reached up and grabbed the thing, light catching the sharp edge of the knife's blade.

The man was still chanting, as I was, and still stroking with his free hand, as I was, but now he paused mid-stroke long enough to bring that knife to his erection and with a quick wrist flick—sliced his flesh.

He flinched with the pain but did not cry out or even stumble in his chanting.

He resumed masturbating and handed the knife back to the cloaked man, who took it to the next kneeling worshipper.

Immediately to my right.

Inside the phallus, the creature—monster—*god*—pushed through a foggy haze laden with moisture. The thing was so close, just on the other side—*inside*—of the phallus. Was this a window into a parallel world, or was it a door? A gateway?

I could make out the thick legs and arms and the chunk of torso and the bulbous head, but there were odd misshapen things protruding off every part of it. I thought of sea creatures in the ocean's depths that look like a child's demented crayon depiction—warped body, gaping mouth, hooked teeth, jagged scales.

What the fuck is that thing?

My fear was now a heavy boulder anchoring me in place.

The man next to me took the knife and cut himself. Didn't even flinch. He resumed jerking off, lubricated now with his blood.

The knife exchanged hands, and then the man was behind me, and the knife handle rested on my shoulder.

My hand reached up all on its own as if compelled to do so, but I stopped it from grabbing the blade. Above the handle, my hand squirmed like a floating spider.

I was not going to cut my dick. No way. No matter what magic these words I was chanting possessed, I was not going to do this.

A voice in my ear: "Slice your penis. Spill your blood."

Not a man's voice.

A woman's.

One I recognized.

The blade handle rested on my shoulder.

I took it and looked up into the woman's face.

I would've expected Margot, of course, lying about not being allowed in here, but it wasn't her.

Dr. Marcia Howler leaned so close her breath warmed my face.

She'd played me. Tricked me.

Led me right to this moment in a room filled with masturbating men and she offering the knife for me to self-mutilate.

Geez, what a crushing blow to such a brilliant man as yourself. Good old Sarcastic Sam back to mock me here at the eleventh hour.

How's the masturbation addiction?

Were these other men her clients as well?

Had they all met Huey Marche, or was he only part of it when an elaborate ruse was needed?

"It is the offering to Onan," she said. "Your *devotion*. Cut yourself."

My hand clamped on the handle and squeezed with all my strength. My arm wanted to move, to bring the blade to my crotch and do as she commanded, to give the blood offering to Onan, to complete the devotion.

The compulsion was so strong, how could I resist?

I was still chanting.

Out of the burning white phallus, the Monster was emerging.

It was not a mirror or a door but folds of curtains squeezed aside into bunches, out of which the creature pushed through a mucusy film.

Birthing from its world into ours.

"It's coming," Howler said, her voice floating with crazed awe.

The chanting grew louder yet, and a man screamed and another and another.

Orgasmic screams.

The monster *was* coming and so were the men.

I might've expected a creature with an oblong penis head and penis arms with spiky hair, some ridiculous creation a teenager would sketch in the margins of a notebook.

This was not that.

What I saw, assuming I saw it at all with the naked, uninebriated eye, was a thing as terrible and disgusting and menacing and horrifying as all those Lovecraftian monsters that could drive you insane if ever you were to look upon them.

A filmy sheen clung to its face like plastic wrap for food and then it tore and sprang back from a head of sharp angles and swollen bumps.

Another man screamed and another.

"Behold," Dr. Howler said and her hood fell back exposing her face. "*Onan!*"

Legs and arms thick and bulbous and a massive chest, this thing could stomp on you like an elephant, leaving you a shattered-bones, flesh-destroyed, bloody mess. But it was such a shock to see this thing at all that you couldn't run if you wanted. Maybe we robed chanters were paralyzed by whatever magic words we were repeating or by whatever hypnotic we were breathing in, but even without those there was no way anyone could flee. The spectacle was just too insane.

Growing off it everywhere like tumors were hands and penises. The hands were chapped raw, the fingers moving like spider's legs. The penises were all erect. Thick blue veins bulged.

A milky glaze engulfed the entire monster. It was crusted over, just like that poor Care Bear beneath my bed, except this thing's bumpy lizard hide was popping pustules of fresh white gunk. Semen. A monster made of spunk continually erupting it all over itself.

The stench was overpowering—a sour, rain-soaked humid stench of ejaculate.

I wanted to vomit. I wanted to scream.

Dr. Howler spread her arms as if welcoming a hug and cried out: "*DEVOTE YOURSELVES! ALL MUST DEVOTE TO ONAN!!!*"

The knife was at my erection.

ShitShitShit

I punched myself just as I had in the car. My head knocked sideways but I was still chanting and the knife blade was still on my dick.

One quick movement was all it would take.

I was going to cut myself. I was going to slice my dick and bleed and then I would come and be one of Onan's disciples forever.

The last of the filmy caul snapped back and the monster—could it actually be Onan, the soul damned to hell for spilling his come on the ground instead of inside his sister-in-law?—emerged completely into the room, hulking there with the blinding white light streaking all around it.

Its face was an eyeless, mouthless terrain of fleshy, gnarled red-flaring knots—*Those're knuckles,* I thought—and then layers peeled apart to become unfolding hands. Each palm chalky and chapped.

Its eyes were protruding erections and its mouth was a tentacle tangle of squirming fingers.

"*ALL MUST WORSHIP BEFORE ONAN!!!*"

The blade at my dick . . .

"*WE ARE IN THE HOUSE OF ONAN!!!*"

My panicked mind worked fast—*House of Onan is the House of All is the place where you surrender ego ego ego ego embrace the ego and paint my name really big but you can't paint or write but you can worship worship yourself I am Michael Stiffe. I am Michael Stiffe. I do NOT humble myself. I do NOT worship you! I WORSHIP MYSELF!!!*

The blade sliced flesh—

"*ARRGHHH!!!*" I hollered, a tumult worthy of a barbarian's battle cry.

And stabbed the knife into my chest.

The blade pierced my left breast and sliced upward to my collarbone. The pain was so much worse than I ever could imagine.

But it worked.

No longer was I chanting or jerking.

The spell, for me at least, was broken.

The monster had not yet made noise and perhaps didn't even have vocal cords, but it produced a sound now, something like a rumbling, crying moan.

And began to turn around toward that light.

A silhouette of wriggling fingers and dicks.

The monster was going back inside the phallus.

Retreating.

Back to whatever world it came from.

"*NO!*" Dr. Howler yelled even louder than I had. "*Damn you! You broke the invocation! YOU BROKE THE DEVOTION!*"

She leaped on me.

I crumpled backwards beneath her, something inside me popping and flooding me with warm pain. She clawed at my face, screaming spittle everywhere, and I tried to grab her and shove her off but she was a writhing beast. A finger found my eye and burrowed into it. Her knee smacked my testicles, my dick a squished slug between us, and the pain in my crotch overtook all other sensations. My vision blanked in a starburst of white. *How's the masturbation addiction?* I bit down into my tongue, *hard*. That brought everything back into focus, and I punched her in the ribs on both sides, again and again. Bones snapped. She screamed through the pain, tried to tear out my eye. Then she grabbed the knife jutting from me and thrusted it in as far as it would go.

Instead of plunging deeper into me and probably killing me, the knife was at a shallow angle and when she shoved the blade, it carved across my collarbone and protruded back out. She stared directly into my eyes, our bodies shoved together, our mouths close enough to kiss, and she yanked the knife to the side. It sliced through my skin to leave a dangling flap, and then she rose up on her knees, straddling me, and gripped the knife in both hands, a vampire assassin about to stake the monster in its coffin.

There was a scream, a *woman's* scream, coming from the other room, and a moment later the door opened and all hell broke loose.

TWENTY-ONE

A FIGURE FILLED THE DOOR.

"Drew!" the woman screamed. "Drew, where are you?"

"Elizabeth?" I asked, so stunned it should've been funny.

"Mike!" she yelled. "Where's Drew? *Drew?!*"

Howler's face contorted, eyes squinting, mouth spasming, and she hissed like a cornered animal.

I punched her in the throat.

She gagged and her whole body jittered. I punched her again, this time in the face. The knife fell from her hands, and I shoved her off me.

Elizabeth entered the room, looking everywhere yet not seeing her husband from all the men in matching robes.

I got to my feet. My robe dangled in tatters. Everything hurt, but I could stand and walk.

Elizabeth grabbed me. Unlike the way her anger could smooth her face into that of a shining rock, her desperate panic bunched it into pale lumps, making her look diseased.

"Where's Drew? *Where is he?*"

"He's right—"

Dr. Howler was back on her feet too. Both hands cupped her throat. When she spoke, she massaged the strangled sound out of it: "Onan would've blessed you. Onan could save you! You could've been *cured!*"

She stumbled toward me.

"What the . . ." Elizabeth was saying.

Howler stumbled another step and stopped.

She started to speak and then threw her arms out from her neck and attacked.

I snatched the knife off the floor and brought it directly up into Howler's plummeting body. The blade pierced right beneath her rib-cage and went upward all the way to the hilt. Hot liquid soaked my hands in a sudden rush, as if I'd ruptured a water balloon of blood inside her.

She made another strangled, gargling groan, eyes slipping to white, and blood dribbled out of her mouth.

"Fuck your therapy," I said.

I almost let her slump to the floor, but then I had a better idea.

The monster was back inside the glowing phallus, the light dim-ming. I lifted Howler, my knife hand pushing inside her body, my other hand grabbing her armpit, and charged forward at the giant dick statue or whatever it was.

She was probably dead already, but I thought she resisted a little, even groaned out a protest, and I shoved her into the phallus. She passed into it and whatever lay beyond as easily as falling into another room. The wet curtain folds of the dimensional portal slipped over her body. She was inside it now, a shadow figure dropping farther away, and the light dimmed out completely, the statue solid once more, and there was only the light from the open doorway and the flicker of all the candles.

The chanting ceased. Still on their knees, the men let their hands fall from their bodies.

"It's over," I said, panting. "The monster's gone. Both of them."

"Drew?" Elizabeth said. "Drew?"

Someone appeared in the doorway.

"You bitch!"

It was Margot. Her mouth and chin were coated with blood.

"Bitch!" she yelled again. "*Bitch! BITCH!*"

Elizabeth turned directly into Margot's punch. It knocked Eliza-beth's head to the side. Margot was still in heels but her business suit was blotched with blood.

"You sucker-punched me," Margot said. "So, I give it right—"

But Elizabeth knocked her mouth shut with a full-arm haymaker.

We men love the idea of a "cat fight," gleefully and stupidly associating it with an aggressive form of lesbianism as well as the exhibitionist potential for ripped clothes and exposed breasts.

In reality, two women fighting is so terribly violent only the sickest mind would find it arousing. Margot returned the punch but it sailed wide and they were caught in an embrace and hit the ground. They screamed and clawed, screeched and slashed, voices strained and bodies writhing—a pair of animals in agonized throes as if poisoned.

The men stood.

They turned in unison to face the spectacle.

They weren't chanting, they weren't masturbating, but their dicks were still hard.

Elizabeth knocked Margot sideways and straddled her. She seized Margot's head with both hands and *thwacked* it hard against the floor. It made a hollow thud.

I'd just murdered someone and shoved her into a parallel dimension, or whatever it was, but watching Elizabeth try to smash Margot's skull into the ground unnerved me so much I felt like vomiting.

It's shock, I told myself. *I need medical attention.*

The men approached in synchronized steps.

Hive mind. They're still under the spell.

Another dull skull thud and Elizabeth sat back.

"Now, where the fuck is my husband?"

He was right there in front of her, approaching in lockstep with the other men.

What were they going to do?

"Elizabeth," I tried to shout, "get out!"

She saw him then but barely got his name out of her mouth before he seized her by the throat and the other men circled around.

The only sound was Elizabeth's struggling cries.

They were going to rape her. I was absolutely sure. Absent their masturbation god, the men were reduced to their most primal urges. They had a woman—two, actually—at their mercy, a thing they would not grant them.

"*Stop!*" I yelled and tried to shove my way through the men, but they were shoulder-to-shoulder, a solid wall. I punched one of them in the spine and he twitched but didn't fall.

I needed something better than my fist.

The knife was gone, of course.

So I grabbed the next best thing—one of the burning candles.

Holding it like a shotgun, I approached the circle again and went for the nearest man.

The flame flickered around his robe's hem and burned out. Shit. Elizabeth cried out again, sounding angry, scared, and defeated. Then the bottom of the robe flared alight and fire climbed up the man's back quickly, as if the fabric were soaked in gasoline.

He might have made a sound but I didn't hear it because he threw his body sideways into another man and one touch of burning robe to more of the same fabric and there were two human-sized torches burning hot and bright. Then three. Then four.

Drew was trying to force himself into his wife's mouth. There was something so robotic about his movements. She beat at his arms, her face turning red.

Another man *Fffooomped* in flames. And another. But Drew kept trying to fuck his wife's mouth.

"*Grab his balls!*" I shouted.

She did—grabbed and *squeezed*.

His scream was the pained whine of a circular saw ripping through wood.

Black, acrid smoke was filling the room and more men were burning. They tried to escape but they kept smacking into each other, tangling, and spreading the fire.

"*Run!*" I yelled.

I grabbed Drew—in the second it took to glance into his face I saw his pupils contract—and pulled him toward the door where Elizabeth was stopped.

"Go!" I shouted. "Go! *Go!*"

A man blocked the way. It was the pale-faced guy who'd made me strip and then told me how he orgasmed watching his father choke to death and how he couldn't watch anyone eat a Drake's Coffee Cake without jerking off and puking.

"No one leaves," he snarled. Sweat dripped off his waxy face. Or maybe it was his skin melting. "*We sacrifice all for Onan!*"

I punched him in the throat.

"You sick fuck," I said, and Elizabeth pushed him out of the way—and into the burning men.

Another smell was overtaking the noxious smoke: the stench of searing flesh and cooking meat.

The three of us lurched out of the worship chamber and I shut the door against the billowing smoke and rising screams.

I almost barricaded them in.

Either way, the door stayed closed, and we got the hell out of there.

By the time we made it back to the lobby, the fire alarm was in full shriek.

Mr. Red Bowtie at reception gawked at us, and then his face changed.

"You're not going anywhere," he said.

From beneath the counter, he raised a sawed-off shotgun.

TWENTY-TWO

HE WALKED AROUND THE COUNTER and approached.

He was maybe ten feet away. I was in front, Elizabeth and Drew behind me.

"Fuck you," I said. "Do it!"

He cocked the shotgun.

Even in the midst of that moment when it was possible I might be killed, a part of my mind wondered how much of our language is derived from male genitalia, or has at least taken on that suggestion.

Cockeyed.

Cockroaches.

Cockiness.

"What happened down there?" Red Bowtie asked over the fire alarm's blare.

None of us said anything. We were breathing heavily, trying to process what the hell had happened.

Cockamamie.

Poppycock.

Cockup.

Out of the stairwell stumbled the tall man who'd been holding

Marche's severed hand. His cloak was singed across his chest, exposing the scorched, bright red flesh beneath. His nose drooped like melting tallow.

He staggered several steps, saw us, and stabbed an accusing finger. "Them!" he shouted. "*Kill them!*"

Red Bowtie and this tall guy, perhaps the cult leader, stared at each other. It was as if they were silently confirming that yes, indeed, they wanted to go through with this.

"Kill them!" he shouted again. "*Onan demands it!*"

Cocksucker.

Cocksure.

I started to turn to simply make a run for it and there was Drew directly behind Red Bowtie.

He'd grabbed the old-fashioned candlestick telephone off the reception desk, and now brought the heavy base of it down directly on Red Bowtie's head.

I swear I heard the hard *thwunk* of it cracking his skull—*Cold-cocked*—but you may not believe me because the moment the phone smashed his head his finger pulled the shotgun's trigger.

He was facing the tall man, and that guy took the shot directly in the chest.

~

We were getting in Elizabeth's car when people on fire ran outside.

She hit the gas and we sped away.

TWENTY-THREE

I WAS IN THE HOSPITAL for three days.

The doctor was an older man with a wry sense of humor. He told me I looked like shit. I told him, "You should see the other guy."

Then he asked if I was in some secret fight club.

"No," I said and grinned. "Masturbation cult."

"At least you don't have a ruptured testicle like another one of my patients," he said.

"That was from the guy's wife," I said.

"Usually is," the doc said.

~

I lucked out: fifty stitches, lots of fluid, antibiotics, and even some pretty good painkillers that dulled the throb in my pelvis where my hip dislocated.

I thought Elizabeth would make the short walk from whatever room Drew was in to mine and, gee, I don't know, thank me, but she didn't.

~

The second night in the hospital, I woke to see someone standing in the doorway.

"Doc?"

The person did not respond. I heard footsteps far down the hall and a machine's steady beep-beep in a nearby room.

"Drew? Elizabeth?"

There was a switch on the wall behind my head to turn on the overhead light, but I couldn't reach it if I tried.

"What do you want?" I asked.

Whoever it was did not say anything and in the blinks between forcing my eyelids back open, the man was gone.

Assuming anyone'd been there at all.

~

A nurse showed me an online article about the fire at the Saint Agnes Hotel. Twelve victims, but the hotel was expected to reopen in two months.

Twelve? Was that all there had been? Or had some survived?

Had the man in the doorway been one of those survivors?

~

The police never questioned me.

~

Huey Marche slouched into my room. I was dressed in hospital sweats that would be added to my bill and waiting for my discharge papers. Marche looked somehow even older, his skinny body bending under the weight of a coat too heavy for the weather.

"Were you watching me last night?"

He sat on the chair by the bed. I was sitting by the window.

"You really fucked up," he said. He was trying to sound angry, but his voice was hoarse, sounding like rocks crumbling against each other.

"You led me to them," I said. "Not my fault."

"'He that worship fully and completely before Onan shall enjoy the exploits of divine revelation. Yet he that rescind or relinquish his fealty shall be punished tenfold in this world and in the next.' So reads The Book of Onan."

"You already told me that."

"You need a reminder." He lifted his stump.

"Why?"

He crossed his skinny legs and propped the stump on his knee. "You're right. It is my fault. I shouldn't've sent you. But it was the only way I could get welcomed back. If I could recruit enough followers to Onan, I could rejoin the fold. I could know that glorious

95

power again. I could be healed."

He suffered a flurry of painful coughs.

"I saw it," I said. "I saw Onan."

His yellowy eyes narrowed.

"Then you know the power. The glory."

"What I know is the stink of semen and charred meat."

He was trying not to cough again and his face sprouted red spots.

"What about the women? Why was Dr. Howler involved? Why Margot?"

"Margot," Huey said with fondness. "Poor girl. She was something special."

"Why would any woman help with this?"

"Power," he said, as if that should've been obvious.

"How many followers are there?"

"I shouldn't be here," Marche said, "but I wanted to warn you. You better watch your back."

"I'm not afraid of them," I said, though my voice wavered a bit.

What if there were many survivors? What if there were hundreds, even thousands of followers?

"You will be," he said. Then he tilted his head and stood. "Or maybe you won't even know. You'll just be dead, and then your *real* punishment will begin."

He slumped to the doorway.

"I don't believe in Hell," I said.

He stopped, glanced back at me, his wrinkled cheeks bunching up toward his eyes. "If you saw Onan, you know Hell is real."

"Hey, Huey," I said. "Good luck with the cancer."

~

When I got home, I went into the bathroom to make sure I could still get it working. A little moisturizer and a few short videos on my iPad and I was back in business.

What if there were other Cults of Onan in the basements of other creepy hotels? What if I was Enemy Number One now? What if they were coming after me?

What if Hell *was* real?

Onan itself had to have been some hallucination—whatever inhalant I was breathing in and the power of suggestion and groupthink.

Chapped hands. Jutting penises. Erupting boils full of ejaculate.

My dick went limp in my hand.

~

Elizabeth, Drew, and Wes moved away. Somewhere south, I think. I called once and Elizabeth said Drew wasn't available to talk. "He's in therapy," she said.

"He'll be okay," I said.

"You know what, Mike? Fuck off."

She hung up.

Catherine never called. Not that I blame her. The house I lived in, and the freedom I had to write every day, was all because in the divorce I walked away with half, and she had a good job and good investments.

~

I was eating lunch, leftover barbecue chicken takeout, and trying to write when someone knocked on the front door.

No one was there, but on the porch was The Book of Onan. It looked like the same one Marche had given me as my entrance ticket, but there could be dozens of copies for all I knew.

Hundreds, maybe.

I reached down to pick it up.

A shadow slipped across the raised outline of the phallus on the cover.

The waxy pale-faced man leaned down toward me. Sunlight streamed around his silhouette, half his face a dried scramble of ruined flesh, right eye a tattered hole, lips desiccated worms. But from those ugly lips came the push of words I heard but didn't understand.

The concrete porch elevatored into my head and everything went dark.

~

Hell is real. If you saw Onan, you know it's real.

I woke with the smell of barbecue in my nostrils. The remainder of my lunch, a half-eaten drumstick, was before me on a plate on my desk. The computer had gone into sleep mode but the Buddy Rich album I'd been listening to kept playing through the speaker.

My pants and underwear were off and my hand was busy stroking my erection.

Shit.

I couldn't feel my dick in my hand. It was all numb.

Shit.

The man with the waxy face that was now burn-scarred and one-eyed stood to my left. His clothes hung off him as if he were a skin-wrapped skeleton. The book was in his hands and he was reading aloud the magic words in a scratchy voice that sounded painful.

Words that were making me masturbate.

Making me worship Onan.

I couldn't stop. Willpower alone would not work. Anger. Fear. None of it mattered. I was slave to the words he was saying, helpless. Doomed.

Were my pupils so large they filled my eyes?

Just another onanistic zombie.

I wasn't tied to my desk chair. Not gagged or blindfolded. None of that was needed when the words themselves were shackles enough.

My dick hurt. The erection was so painful. It was the sort I used to suffer as a teenager when it seemed my entire self was reduced to my privates and I had to run to the bedroom or bathroom to let out the tidal wave of come.

Except this time it wasn't blue balls hurting me.

I hurt because this was my punishment.

I'd failed to complete the devotion to Onan, and now I would suffer as he had when God cast judgment upon his failure to impregnate his brother's wife.

This so angered the Lord he slew Onan.

I was going to come, only it wouldn't be ejaculate—it would be blood. Lots and lots of blood.

He paused and his one eye looked at me.

The yellowy bloodshot eyeball was a slippery, ugly thing squeezed inside crinkled folds of hardened flesh.

And in that eye, I saw only madness.

There were no other disciples of Onan, at least not hunting me down. No secret cults in other hotel basements. Or if there were, they didn't know about me or didn't care. Had they, they'd be here too, staging an elaborate seance or sacrifice or both.

No, it was only this guy, deranged to begin with after witnessing his father's death as he had his first orgasm, and now gone completely insane.

That eye dropped back to the book, but instead of continuing with the words he lifted from inside the book a cleaver. Sunlight starbursted along the blade's edge. Then the words resumed.

As did my hand.

With my other hand, I willed my fist into my face.

My head knocked to the side but I kept stroking. I punched myself again. And again. Didn't matter. I felt my face stinging into what would be bruises, if I lived long enough, but my other hand did not stop.

I tried once more, a punch as hard as I could, but again there was no luck.

He's not going to kill me. He's only going to chop off my hand. I can write one-handed. I can certainly jerk off one-handed.

What if he severed both?

Be hard to pray with no hands, if you know what I mean.

What if he cuts off something else?

Be such a sinner, and we must take your manhood.

My insides liquified.

I'd never been so terrified.

Except—

Except ego could save me again. *I do NOT worship Onan! I worship myself!*

The trance started to let go, I felt myself in my hand, but I couldn't make myself stop.

Embrace the ego, Marshall said.

How?

Don't know. Paint my name really big?

I couldn't do that, but I didn't need to.

On the wall to my right was the framed page from *Publisher's Weekly*.

Michael Stiffe aspires toward the literary perversions of a Roth or an Updike or even an Irving, yet resigns himself comfortably to being merely perverted.

That framed quote—a backhanded kind of praise in a snarky, derisive tone—had been my favorite go-to porn for years.

How many times had I stared at that quote with my dick in hand? Jerking off is a solitary, self-worshiping endeavor as it is, but doing it to your own picture or, say, a published quote of near-praise about your work, well, that's another level of narcissism altogether. But the moment my eyes fell upon that oft-admired quote, I felt my hand, felt myself wrapped in my hand.

I was all dick. All ego.

The trance was broken.

I could've grabbed a pen out of the mug on my desk or even the little metal ruler I had for making annotations, but instead I grabbed the half-eaten drumstick off my plate and attacked.

I moved so fast he couldn't react, and he was still saying whatever bizarro words were in that book, so the drumstick went right into his mouth.

His remaining eye went so big with surprise I thought it might pop right out of his head, and then he was gagging on the drumstick and I knocked out his legs and drove him to the floor. The cleaver jumped out and clattered nearby. He squirmed beneath me, arms and legs flailing in every direction. He was a pinned bug.

The drumstick was hitting the back of his throat. I wedged it in harder. Leaned with all my weight. His whole body convulsed. Phlegmy mucus wormed down the sides of his cheeks. Beneath the crumple-hardened skin of his face blushed crimson islands in a pale-flesh ocean.

"Sorry it's not Drake's," I said through clenched teeth. "Choke on it! Like father, like son!"

You can't kill him, idiot. What the hell will you do with the body?

I wish I could say my thinking was more humane—*Killing people is wrong,* or at least, *You already killed one person, isn't that bad enough?*—but it was much more selfish. Whatever voice it was in my head, Sarcastic Sam or my good old conscience, that made the point about corpse disposal, it was enough to make me let up, and that was enough for the guy to fight back.

He kneed me in the crotch and smack-punched my face at the same time. I tumbled off him and he spit out the drumstick.

I brought my hands up in defense, but he wasn't about to attack—he snatched up The Book of Onan and staggered out of the office and broke into a run down the hall and out the front door.

My breathing was hard and fast. I should go after the guy, not to kill him, though the cleaver winked sunshine at me, but to hold him captive until the police could arrest him. I yanked up my underwear and pants and tried to stand. And that's when I heard it.

The screaming muffler-howl of a teenager driving way too fast.

Who knows why anything happens. Random chance? Destiny? Doesn't matter.

Sometimes the exact right thing happens exactly when it should.

I made it to my office window in time to see my attacker mid-air above the piss-colored hatchback that hadn't slowed at all when a burned-faced, crazed disciple of Onan ran out into the street.

The hatchback skidded to an asphalt-burning, zigzagging stop, and the guy in the air hit the road with a skull-cracking thwack.

~

When the police arrived, the teenage driver finally pried his hands off the wheel and tried to hug himself steady, his face shocked, his eyes tearing.

"You saw what happened?" the cop asked me.

"Guy ran right out into the road," I said. "He might've been suicidal."

The cop gestured to the thing under my arm. "What's that?"

I pretended to be surprised. "Oh, just a book. I was reading when it happened."

~

That should've put an end to things.

A few days later, I drove back to that roadside antique shop. If the old guy was still there, I'd give him back The Book of Onan, tell him I didn't want any more trouble, and wish him all the best (only a little sarcastically) with his cancer.

No speeding hatchback hurtled into me, but coincidence or fate or whatever must have a good sense of humor.

On the dusty glass counter in the back was another pulp paperback with a sultry woman on the cover.

"Humble yourself," I said. "Hey, Huey, you here?"

I walked around the counter.

"Maybe back here jerking—"

And stopped.

Someone was on the floor in the back room. Not moving.

I reached in and found the light switch.

Huey Marche was on the floor. He was dead, a stone phallus jutting from his mouth, his pants at his ankles, his crotch a slaughtered, bloody mess.

And his other hand was amputated.

Somewhere, in a basement in a creepy hotel perhaps, a man or even a bunch of men in graduation-like gowns are offering an old man's severed hand, dick, and balls to a god made of penises and semen.

I managed to get outside to puke, doing it next to the giant wooden spool.

A car pulled in and I was sure it was an Onan disciple. They'd come back for something and when they saw me they would drag me inside and do me like they'd done Huey.

Except it wasn't one of the black-cloaked Onanists. It was the Good News woman. She got out of her car and appreciated me a moment, still bent over and spitting.

"Are you okay?" Her makeup had yet to crumble.

"Is that what you'd say to a man in a burning building?"

She chuckled like I'd made quite the amusing joke.

I guess she'd forgotten all about how mean and awful I was.

"More good news?" I asked and pointed at the pamphlet in her hand.

"Same as always," she said.

"The Lord is risen," I said.

"Yes, indeed."

She handed me the pamphlet. On the cover, a well-dressed family prayed in a splash of sunlight cutting through heavenly clouds.

"You can be saved," she said. "There's still time."

"Not for everyone," I said. "You don't want to go in there."

"It's okay," she said. "His judgment cometh."

"Huey's dead in there. Mutilated."

She glanced at the antique shop, clucked her tongue, and turned back to me. "Of course he is. It is God's will."

"He was murdered."

"Did you do it?"

"What? No."

She shrugged. "Then you have nothing to worry about. Do you?"

"Hold on, you're not freaked out by what I'm telling you?"

"Only the disbeliever is shocked by God's mighty judgment. All things serve His will, even you. And me, of course."

I saw it in her face then, a knowledge of things she'd deny. What I'd taken as the expression of the typical religious idiot was actually a facade for something far worse.

"You were spying on him," I said. "Was it for Dr. Howler? Was she the one in charge of it all?"

"In charge? Why, God is the one in charge. How silly to think otherwise."

"Onan? *That* god?"

"There's only *one* God. All others serve Him and Him alone."

I was completely sure this unassuming middle-aged woman with bad makeup and religious aphorisms had been working with the Onan cultists in some way. Marche was ousted, and this woman had been sent to keep tabs.

"And when I came here and you grabbed my wrist, you were expecting me. Howler told you about me, about my wife leaving me."

"All things serve the Lord," she said in a disgustingly cheerful way.

"He works in mysterious ways, huh?" I said and dropped the pamphlet.

She wagged a finger. "We don't question God. We just obey."

~

I heard the barking and went to my office window.

Marshall emerged from his van and three dogs leaped out after him and ran around my front lawn, chasing each other, tails wagging.

He slid open the side door and when he emerged again, he had a puppy cuddled against his chest.

~

I named the puppy Onan.

Eventually, he'll learn to follow my commands.

~

I kept the book. Holy Viagra might prove useful.

If more Onan worshippers are out there, they might eventually find me, but I'll be ready for them. With both hands.

Yet, I have learned something.

If there is a lesson, it is simply this: I'd let my life get out of hand. Go on and laugh. Someone should. Even as I thought I was taking action to do something good—finding Drew to bring him back to his family—I was being manipulated by other forces.

And those forces almost killed me.

Jerking off is its own kind of force. A compulsion to which you can be master or servant.

It's about self-control.

Dr. Howler would be proud.

This story, you see, is the first thing I've finished writing in years. Electronic folders with half-completed and barely started manuscripts clutter my hard drive.

It takes a long time to finish a book when you're constantly masturbating.

I've put my dick back in my pants.

I'm not going to swear off masturbation forever, that strikes me as its own sort of cultish philosophy, but a little self-control is worth practicing.

AUTHOR'S NOTE AND ACKNOWLEDGEMENTS

When asked where I get my story ideas, I often have only a faint notion that does little to satisfy the questioner. For this story, I may have an actual answer.

At some point in the last year, I wrote the line "Puberty made me a writer," and a few weeks later had almost 20,000 words of a novella about a writer who finds a haunted short story that traps anyone reading it in a masturbatory trance.

I liked the narrator, he was both witty and self-deprecating, but the story wasn't quite working so I set it aside.

In July of 2022, Bleeding Edge Books published my novella *Children of Fire*. In it, an ex-detective is hired by his ex-wife's new husband to rescue their child from a religious cult in Western New York.

I've long been fascinated by religion and religious cults. *Children of Fire* gave me an opportunity to explore that fascination. It's a good story, intense and emotional but also funny, I think, particularly when the narrator throws sarcastic quips at the cult leader.

All literary works have their influences, some direct and some incidental.

Several years ago, Joe Hill published *Strange Weather*, a collection of four novellas. One of them is *Rain*, an end-of-the-world tale in which crystallized nails fall from the sky. He wrote it, he says, as a spoof of his novel *The Fireman*.

That gave me an idea. What if I took my unfinished novella—its working title, *Puberty Writer*—and wrote it as a parody of *Children of Fire*? Instead of dealing with a haunted story that makes you masturbate, the narrator will have to infiltrate a masturbation cult. What could be more outlandish and ridiculous than that? I wrote the first draft in a month and had a great time doing it. At some point, the story became less ridiculous and more upsetting, unnerving, and downright horrifying. I hope you agree.

The short story "The Sins of Louanna and Ray," which Mike blames as the final nail in the coffin of his marriage, is something I wrote a few years ago. It's a direct response to Peter Straub's "The Ballad of Ballard and Sandrine" and Paul Bowles's "A Distant Episode." My story—in this case, Mike's story—is nowhere near as unsettling as either of those two masterworks, but I think it's creepy and disturbing and I'm delighted to see it published.

Many times while writing *The Hands of Onan*, I wondered if anyone would ever want to read it, much less publish it.

It's a ridiculous, silly story. Yet it's also terrifying. People are often willing, even eager, to believe anything. Remember Heaven's Gate? Those followers believed they were going to ride the Hale-Bopp Comet into a higher state of evolutionary existence.

Life is scary. Religions and cults promise security, peace, prosperity, and hope for what might await after death. All you have to do is surrender. The worshippers of Onan get the extra benefit of sexual self-gratification.

For me, nothing is scarier than fanaticism, be it religious, political, or ideological (or masturbatory). This novella gave me yet another opportunity to explore the dangers of such zealotry.

I am thrilled and honored to have Grindhouse Press publish my story. They're one of the coolest small horror presses around. Immense thanks are due to Carrie Nicely and the entire team at Grindhouse. Their work on this book improved the story and has given it a chance to find an audience. Special shoutout to the awesome people I met at Scares that Care Charity Weekend VIII. It was a blast. The horror community is the best.

Along with *Where do you get your ideas?*, people sometimes ask if the characters and events in my books are based on real people and actual experiences.

Some questions, especially in this case, are best left unanswered.

Thank you for reading. I wish you well.

Chris DiLeo
September 2022

Chris DiLeo is the author of several books, including *Dead End* from JournalStone, *Revival Road* from Bloodshot Books, and *Children of Fire* from Bleeding Edge Books. He is a high school English teacher in New York. Follow him @authordileo.

Other Grindhouse Press Titles